THE GLORIOUS ONES

THE GLORIOUS ONES

A NOVEL

FRANCINE PROSE

OPEN ROAD

INTEGRATED MEDIA

NEW YORK

Copyright © 1974 by Francine Prose

Cover design by Jason Gabbert

ISBN 978-1-4804-4542-0

This edition published in 2013 by Open Road Integrated Media, Inc.
345 Hudson Street
New York, NY 10014
www.openroadmedia.com

To my family

THE GLORIOUS ONES

1 • ARMANDA RAGUSA

IN THE MIDDLE OF THE JOURNEY OF OUR LIFE, I came to myself in a dark forest. Wild boars lined the wayside, gnashing at my feet. Hissing adders, looped around the branches, spat venom in my face. But I, Flaminio Scala, the Captain, Prince of Warriors, Bravest of the Brave, First to Battle, Last to Flee—I, Flaminio Scala, the most courageous man in Christendom—I, Flaminio Scala, was not afraid.

Slicing through the underbrush with my sword, I forged ahead until the road I traveled forked in two. And there, at that dim parting of the ways, I encountered a most amazing phenomenon.

One of the paths was marked "Fame," the other, "Obscurity."

"Virgin Mary the Whore!" I cried, running headlong down the trail which seemed to promise my heart's dearest wish. Yet soon my characteristic prudence and intelligence caused me to reconsider:

It was all too simple, too perfect; I sensed a trap.

Slowly, cautiously, I traced my way back to the fork—where, now, a small, fair-haired boy was seated on a granite boulder.

"What is the trick?" I asked him, assuming, of course, that he would know.

"There is no trick," he replied, with a smile of angelic sincerity. "Go whichever way you please."

For some reason, I believed him, and continued on my journey. I became famous, and believed him until the moment of my death. But here, in this old prison, where unremitting contentment makes the very saints long for hell, I have begun to understand the trick.

I see now that the boy was Francesco Andreini, and that his reassurance was only the first of many deceptions. And, looking down from above, I can finally see the true way of those paths.

I have learned that both roads, followed long enough, eventually merge in the same dank, overgrown swamp of Obscurity.

How disquieting, this new knowledge of mine! How clever of the gods, to have devised such a perfect punishment for Flaminio Scala!

Each day, I contemplate the future of the world, and my stomach starts to churn. I see us dead, discarded, our spirits parodied by wooden marionettes. Perhaps you might think that the peace of heaven would have tempered my desire for eternal fame. But it is not that way.

And that is the reason I am troubling you on this hot, sticky evening, Armanda, in this dream which causes you to toss and moan. Remembering your beautiful spirit, I am inclined to think that you are the only one among them who might still heed my voice. I pray that you still remember me—my handsome face, my figure, the touch of my hands on that night we spent so sweetly in each other's arms. I pray that, in recalling that night, you will see it as our secret, our password—by which you may know that the voice in this vision cannot be that of an impostor.

For now, after so many years of silence, I would like to give you one last direction.

Remember our history, Armanda, and write it down—in

detail, not in outline, as we used to plan the scenes. Make the others promise to say it again and again, to tell it to their children and grandchildren, to anyone who will listen. Collect every remnant and memento of our great career. Keep them with you all your life, then entrust them to a monastery, for safekeeping.

Then, if we are lucky, the memory of Flaminio Scala and his Glorious Ones will not vanish so quickly from the earth.

That was my vision of you, Flaminio Scala. I woke up sweating, the blood frozen solid in my veins. "Captain!" I screamed. "Is that you, crouching near the door? Are you making those rustling noises in my trunk?"

Yet I knew that the room was empty, and the trunk was full of mice. Longing to find you in another dream, I closed my eyes; but I could not sleep.

Flaminio Scala, I thought, how clever of you to call on me. Who else but Armanda Ragusa would be lying awake like this, straining to see your face in the darkness? And how wise of you to see that Armanda Ragusa was the only one worthy of your trust. Who else owes you such a debt?

Rest easy, Captain, you can rely on me to obey your last command. For, if I failed you now, it would mean that I had forgotten how you saved me from the Orphanage of the Blessed Brides of Christ. And how could I forget the man who rescued me from a place in which small children were obliged to spend the nights of Lent in stone coffins lined with moss?

You think heaven is a prison, Flaminio? At the convent orphanage, we longed for heaven; in contrast to our earthly home, it seemed like a circus of sinful delights. Imagine what it was like for us there: endless granite corridors, dripping wet. Pale tapers, glowing dimly in the chapel. Ice water from the well. Stiff, starched linen.

Now imagine what it was like for us to see you and The Glorious Ones for the first time! You were so beautiful! We had never seen anyone like you before! On that bright October morning, as we stood in the courtyard, watching you come up the road, our eyes bulged out, our knees buckled with awe!

Imagine, Flaminio: in that world of coarse, black smocks and grey vestments, the only colors we had ever seen were the blue of the sky, the green of leaves, the pink of our own mouths. And suddenly, out of nowhere, you and The Glorious Ones were riding toward us with those scarlet hose, those violet capes, those emerald velvet caps with peacocks' plumes. Your horses had silver ribbons plaited in their tails; your brilliant, silken banners fluttered in the wind.

And the women? My God, they were dressed in gowns of orange and red striped satin! Could those creatures really have belonged to the same race as our prioress?

Imagine: in the convent, we had been taught that a mouth open in laughter was a mouth pursed to receive the devil's kiss. Yet you were all laughing, chattering, reaching out to touch each other's bodies. One of the younger men spurred his horse and galloped in a circle away from the procession; smiling, the women tossed back their heads, and the sparkle of their earrings blinded us like suns.

The girls of the orphanage truly believed that each lascivious thought fueled the fires of hell for ten thousand years—imagine the commotion which began when we noticed those giant codpieces, those half-naked breasts!

But gradually, as you drew nearer, we all fell silent.

You were riding in front, Flaminio, shouting commands and brandishing your sabre in the air. You sat up very straight, and, beneath the gold braid and silver medals, your chest seemed eight feet wide. Your arms were thicker than my body; I could have crawled into your full, black beard and hidden. Your face astounded me; your fierce eyes made my heart beat fast, as if I were in danger.

At first, I assumed that other orphans were all staring at you, that you were the cause of that stillness which had fallen over the courtyard. Then, I realized that they had not even noticed you, for their gaze never left the woman who was riding just behind you. Is it her beauty which so fascinates them, I wondered—her blood-red lips, her low-cut bodice, that gleaming mane of curly hair which covers her like a cloak? A moment later, I understood.

Whenever the jogging of her mare caused the woman's hem to rise and sway, the orphans of the Blessed Brides of Christ were treated to an unmistakable glimpse of pink lace stockings!

Pink lace stockings! How could they have imagined such a thing—those orphaned girls, whose feet burned perpetually in those rough wool socks!

"Ah," murmured one of the older girls at last, "Now I know who that is. It is the Whore of Babylon, and the Company of the Damned."

"No," hissed Mother Maria Rosaria, our prioress, as she herded us inside the convent. "It is something much worse. It is a company of actors—the most devious and clever of all Satan's minions."

"In that case," I answered, "hell must surely be a pleasant place to live." I was famous for contradicting everything the Mother Superior said.

But, if I did not believe the prioress then, I almost believed her half an hour later, when she emerged from a brief interview with you, and announced that we would soon be permitted to witness a special performance by Flaminio Scala and his Glorious Ones.

What happened in that barren cell, Flaminio? Did you really bewitch Maria Rosaria? Is that what caused her face to shine with such pleasure? Could you possibly have cuckolded the Lord of heaven?

I never asked you, Captain, I never knew. But, over the years, my curiosity and my weakness for daydreaming have led me to compose this small scenario.

As the play begins, Flaminio Scala is standing stage right, beneath an iron crucifix. A moment later, the prioress enters the room.

She is a dour, forbidding woman; her wide, puffy face is perfectly expressionless, enlivened only by the occasional spasms of a sharp, nervous squint. Beneath her swollen lids are the cold blue eyes of a rat. Her body is massive, broad-shouldered, muscular; as she lumbers towards you, her step seems so graceless and ungainly that the audience begins to wonder if she is really a man in disguise, and a few brave spectators start to giggle.

Bowing dramatically, Flaminio Scala strides across the cell to greet her, but she shrinks back, as if in terror. "I cannot imagine," she whispers, in a voice so low that the audience must lean forward to hear, "why you have come to trouble our peace. In this convent, we drape black curtains over our windows to keep out the sight and sounds of men. Why, men, should I let my charges witness your filthy antics?"

Suddenly, Flaminio Scala falls to his knees. Grabbing the hem of the prioress' robe, he strikes his forehead on the granite floor. There is blood on his face, tears stream down his cheeks.

"Mother," he sobs, "have pity on me. I was once a lover of God, like yourself. Yet I let myself be lured down the path of temptation, abandoned in the forest of wickedness. Now, I stand before you, teetering on the precipice above the valley of despair. I feel that I have been cursed for eternity, doomed to a horrible fate.

"If your innocent heart could comprehend an actor's existence, you would know: by now, my sins are so enormous that no ordinary absolution could help me. If I had a mountain of gold, I would build the most exquisite cathedral in God's kingdom. Were I a sculptor, I would carve a statue of Mary Magdalene, to remind Jesus of His love for repentant sinners. But I, Flaminio Scala, the most desperate man in Christendom, have none of those things.

"Forgive me, Mother. I have nothing to offer Him but my art, and the desire to provide some innocent pleasure for His most unfortunate children. And I truly believe that you are the one to help me—you, Maria Rosaria, God's dearest bride, a holy sister of compassion and mercy."

Flaminio's pleas go on and on. Neither Mother Maria Rosaria nor anyone in the audience knows whether to believe him. But no one would dare doubt him enough to take responsibility for his soul.

By the time he has finished speaking, the prioress is convinced that she is a saint of redemption, and a woman of exquisite beauty.

But on the day you visited the orphanage, Captain, I had not yet made up that play. All I knew was that something very strange was happening in our convent.

The nuns and the other girls—fools that they were—still believed that there were demons within our walls. Despite the prioress' efforts to calm them, they giggled frantically and squawked like barnyard hens. A long time passed before they were able to reassure each other that the devils were not particularly ferocious; by then, you and The Glorious Ones had already built the platform in the courtyard, and begun your play.

Eventually, however, the girls of the convent were clearly enjoying your comedy. They howled with delight when those masked old men raced around the stage, smacking each other with huge rubber bats; they cooed with sympathy when the hero lost all the money he had saved for his starving mother. They were surprised, but not alarmed, when the crescent moon floated down from the sky, bearing the pink-stockinged woman on its back. After all, they knew that devils could do anything!

And I, Flaminio? I must confess that I remember very little of that performance; yet I can recall every word of your speeches.

"I have trekked across the deserts of Araby," you declaimed. "I have fought the fanged snake-men of Patagonia. I have bargained with the thousand-thumbed merchants of Morocco. But never in all my travels have I encountered a race of misers like the Italians."

You see, I do remember: you were playing the Captain, trying to cheat Pantalone out of his gold. But the truth was that you were my entire cast, my plot, my dialogue, my setting; when you were gone from the stage, I dreamed of the scenes in which you would return. Sitting on the cold flagstones, I stared hard at you, tense with concentration—as if I could have reached you with some power from my eyes. And I thought to myself: who else but a fool like Armanda Ragusa would have gone so lovesick over the first handsome man she had ever seen?

Then, at the very end of the play, something occurred which actually convinced me that the prioress had been right all along. I began to shake with terror, for I knew that I had lost my heart to a demon.

The other actors had left the stage; the nuns and orphans were cheering and applauding. All alone, you strode to the front of the platform, and bowed to us.

"I thank you for your kindness," you said, "and for your help in lightening my burden of sin. But, most of all, I would like to thank the Blessed Mother Maria Rosaria for having permitted me to adopt one of her precious charges into my troupe."

"So he has talked the prioress into letting him take one of us!" I thought. "Then the power of Satan is a million times greater than anything I'd suspected!"

Yet, all of a sudden, I did not care if my savior was a demon; and, from then on, it was the old fairy tale come true for me.

Do you know the story of the Princess in Rags, Flaminio? Her enemies, the wicked courtiers, imprison her in a coalbin when the handsome prince arrives to choose a wife. The girls of the palace are paraded before him, but he rejects them, one by one, until—drawn by some mysterious and irresistible force— he moves through the castle and finds his destined mate.

"I want that one," you said, pointing towards the corner in which the nuns were holding me back.

And did I glide from my dungeon with the grace and presence of a natural-born queen? Did I greet you with the sweet half-smile of a goddess receiving her due? No, Captain, you know I did not. My mouth fell open; I felt dizzy, nauseated, sick; I tripped and stumbled my way across the courtyard, until, at last, I stood on stage, between you and the prioress. I was trembling, straining to understand: why in the world had you chosen me?!

Mother Maria Rosaria was asking you the same question, as she held me by the shoulder with such distaste that her great meaty hand felt like dust on my sleeve.

Of course, she could hardly demand to know why you had chosen the ugliest girl in the convent; no one in the convent was supposed to notice things like ugliness. Instead, she quietly suggested that perhaps you might be better pleased by one of the more devout young women. And she mentioned a beautiful girl whom I hated for her clear blue eyes and thick black hair.

"On the contrary, Mother Superior," you replied, running your eyes over my body like the coarse brushes with which the nuns made us scrub. "This one is perfect. How old is she?"

"About fourteen," answered the prioress.

"Just as I thought," you cried. "And yet, who would ever think to call this specimen a woman? Look at her flat chest, her short, stubby body, her rubbery skin! Look at that strawlike hair, those wandering, half-crossed eyes, that moustache on her upper lip! Perhaps, if we are lucky, she will grow a beard like mine.

"Yes, this beauty suits my needs perfectly. Even without a mask, she will have my audience howling with laughter. And certainly, I could parade her naked across the stage, and the blessed pope himself would never accuse me of sins against chastity!"

Sweet Jesus, Flaminio! What devil prompted you to say those

things? Did you think I had no heart, no mind? Did you believe that a body like mine could not have a soul?

I think you knew the truth, Captain, you with your famous eye for character. But why, why did you insult me that way?

For five years, I asked myself that question, day after day after day. I whispered it into the mirror when I put on my makeup; I pestered the gypsies we met on the road. Sometimes, when I shrieked and somersaulted on stage, it was all an effort to drive the sound of it from my ears. For five years, that question echoed in my mind so loudly that I never heard the cheering, the applause. And yet, when I finally found the courage to speak it aloud, I whispered as softly as if I were at confessional, in church.

Remember? It was the first thing I asked you on that morning I awoke to find you beside me. How strange! That question seemed so important that it kept me from saying how much you had pleased me; it kept me from thanking you for having reconciled me with my own flesh. Tell me, Flaminio—if I had said those things, would that have persuaded you to spend a little longer in my bed?

But this is what I said: "Flaminio Scala," I asked, "why did you say those terrible things about me, that day you saved me from the convent?"

For a moment, you looked startled, confused. Then you sighed, and kissed me tenderly on the forehead.

"Ah, my darling Armanda," you said. "If only you had asked me earlier. How easily I could have explained this matter, which has obviously caused you great pain and confusion. For as always, the truth is far prettier than these loathsome scenarios we enact.

"Rest easy, my dear. I only invented those lies to expose the hypocrisy of that vain and silly nun. I assure you, Armanda, my decision had nothing to do with your physical appearance. No, the real reason I chose you for my troupe was this.

"Even in that crowd of ragged, pitiful orphans, your beautiful spirit shone through to me with an almost blinding light. It was a vision of sorts, Armanda, a vision which I have never forgotten. Over the years, it has given me hope, inspiration, and the courage to keep myself chaste. But it has also intimidated me, and kept me from declaring my perfect love.

"Finally, last night, I could stand it no longer. Searching for that pure light, I forced myself on you with bestial rudeness. And now, I am wondering: how can I *ever* make you forgive me?"

"There is no need to apologize," I answered coldly. "You were not the first one. There is a shortage of women in this troupe."

By then, you see, all my pride was back. For I had not wanted you to say any of those things, Flaminio, I had no desire to hear your praises of my soul. I had wanted you to tell me that my face and body were ethereally lovely, painfully beautiful! But how could I have expected you to lie?

And so I settled for something less, and made it suffice: I settled for your vision of my beautiful soul.

Are you wondering why I believed you, when I had heard so many of your lies? I swear to you, Captain: it was not the heat of love which convinced me, but the cold argument of logic. For once, I had no cause for doubt: what else but the folly of passion could have brought you to the bed of a woman like me? And it was true that you had kept yourself chaste. If you had ever paid the slightest notice to the crazy women who pressed their bodies against you after the performances, Armanda Ragusa would have been the first to see. Had you loved another actress in our troupe, I would have killed her with my taunts, my vicious tongue, my only weapons: you know me, Flaminio.

But, with no reason to doubt, I believed in your vision of my beautiful soul. It gave me back my pride, and helped me restrain myself from asking you why, after that one night, you never came to my bed again. Instead of tormenting you with my love-sickness, I took to staring at you, to watching your every move on stage, just as I had done that morning at the convent. And sometimes, sometimes Flaminio, I fancied that I could see your vision of my beautiful spirit, burning deep behind your eyes.

Now listen to me, listen to the way I have told this tale: One summer night, a man named Flaminio Scala slept in the arms of the homeliest woman in Europe. Surely, the Captain would never have bothered to visit my dreams if this were the greatest glory of his life; surely, there were finer moments in his career. Of course there were! Flaminio Scala, the leader of The Glorious Ones, was a man of history! And it is for the sake of that history that I will stop this foolish woman's dreaming, and begin again.

But how, exactly, to begin? Shall I repeat the Captain's own account of his early years?

"My friends," he told us one night, after a week of shoddy performances, "I started in life as a master criminal, a confidence man, a swindler. One day, languishing in prison, I searched my brain for some way of putting my natural dishonesty to some honest use, and walked out of jail an actor."

Yet why should Armanda Ragusa help spread these lies? Flaminio Scala was never a bandit—he was merely seeking some clever new way of insulting his troupe. I laughed, to show him that I understood the joke; in fact, I knew the joke was more absurd than even he would have admitted.

Flaminio Scala could never have fooled me. I had not forgotten the fierce eyes of the young priests who sometimes came to help with convent business; and as soon as I saw those eyes in the Captain's face, I knew that it had begun for him in the seminary.

Still, I must confess some difficulty in seeing him there—Flaminio, with his boasts and his swagger. But perhaps that was the way with all the students who were troubled by what the theologians referred to as "doubts."

Doubts! Those priests could never speak the language. Flaminio and his friends had no doubts—they were fighting for their lives!

Late at night, huddled in the damp cold cells, they were struggling to save that part of themselves which the priests wished so badly to destroy—that part of themselves which still loved the beauties of the earth. In the course of that battle, the acting began—the jokes, the songs, the dances, the innocent showing-off. Soon, it had become a craft for them, and, hour after hour, they labored to perfect the cruelty and precision with which they imitated their professors. At the start, they spoke in whispers, for fear of offending the others. Then, one night, they could no longer resist the temptation to speak out loud.

The stage is set to resemble a school chapel. Alone in the confessional, a young priest shivers in the December chill, awaiting the midnight bells which will permit him to return to his cell.

Flaminio Scala enters stage left, swaggering in a manner designed to show the audience that he is up to something; the encouragements of his friends are protecting him like a suit of armor. He kneels gracefully, presses his lips against the smooth wood of the confessional, and begins to speak:

"Father," he whispers, then stops, struggling to contain his laughter. "Father," he continues, in a steadier tone, "I am begging your forgiveness, though I myself am not quite sure if I have sinned."

"Most likely you have," replies the priest, recognizing the voice of his most rebellious student.

"No," Flaminio murmurs intensely. "It is not what you think. It is something much more serious, more perilous. Listen: over the past few months, I have been wrestling with the conviction that I myself am the Lord Jesus Christ Almighty, returned to usher in the Judgment."

"You are talking nonsense," the priest answers nervously.

"And so it was that you doubted me the first time!" Flaminio Scala cries, in a voice so majestic, commanding, and ominous that the altar, painted on the backdrop, begins to pitch and sway.

The young confessor is trembling now. Has he heard the voice of God? "Tell me more," he whispers, clutching the inside of the confessional door.

Flaminio Scala tells him more. In a calm, authoritative tone, he speaks to him of life terrestrial and life divine. He laments his fifteen hundred years of exile, recalls all the agony of his passion. As he describes the unimaginable sweetness of his seat at God's right hand, his words seem to swell and resound like the notes of an organ.

Just before the curtain comes down on this scene, a few members of the audience notice that the priest has begun to weep.

In a brief epilogue, set on the next morning, Flaminio and three accomplices are expelled for their sinful and blasphemous defiance of the First Commandment.

Armanda Ragusa, I ask myself, what sort of lover are you, to take such delight in the image of your beloved and his friends scrambling for pennies, fishing breadcrumbs from the canals of Venice? What sort of woman are you, to have such contempt for those four spoiled children, so unwilling to dirty their hands with honest labor? And yet, I am not so unlike them that I cannot understand: they had just escaped from prison! They wanted to be free!

And so Flaminio and his companions came to devise the perfect plan. They would support themselves with the same spoiled foolishness which had so amused them in the seminary—they would be actors! Unburdened by rehearsals, repetition, scripts, their wit would be the freshest thing in Venice! They needed no leaders, no direction, no prearranged dialogue—they would improvise! The plazas of the city would be their stage, their audience—the people of the street! How could they possibly fail!

What sort of woman am I, to imagine the enthusiasm in their voices, and feel such bitterness?

Yet perhaps my sin is only the simple, understandable envy of easy success. For, as it happened, Flaminio and his friends proved absolutely right. In no time, they were drawing huge crowds, swarms of urchins, messenger boys on errands, cooks on their way to market, merchants' sons walking home from school. Young men told their mistresses, children brought their friends; distant acquaintances stopped each other on the street to describe Flaminio's antics. The people of Venice were desperate for entertainment, and the actors' caps grew heavy with coins.

Sometimes, I wonder why Flaminio never spoke of those days with fondness and nostalgia. Surely, it was the only time in his career when he was not alone on top, alone with the worries of a leader. Surely, he was happier then, when there was no Andreini to plague him with vicious tricks.

But all he ever told us was the story of his friends' destruction, that gruesome tale which he repeated again and again, like a litany, a sermon against the sins of recklessness and disloyalty.

"One March evening," the Captain used to say, "myself and three companions were invited to perform before the Doge of Venice. In retrospect, I see that it was the end of the social season, and the Duke had invited a few stray guests whom he deemed unworthy of anything more than some local amateur talent. But then, I was not yet a man of deep wisdom and wide experience, fully conversant with the subtle machinations of the aristocratic mind; then, I was merely a poor, ambitious boy, who mistook the doors of that gilded hall for the very portals of Paradise.

"With characteristic good sense, I suggested that I play the Crafty Venetian, and that my friends enact the Three Roman Thieves. The courtiers were cool at first, but, gradually, as it became apparent that I would consistently trick and frustrate that absurd trio of scoundrels, the Duke began to bellow with laughter and beat his fat fists on the table.

" 'One Venetian outwitting three Romans! What patriotism! What wit!' What could have pleased His Excellence more! We were a brilliant success—so brilliant, in fact, that, at the end of the play, the Duke offered to reward the author of our comedy with a hundred pounds of gold!

"Watching the nobleman's wet, snarling lips, I realized that he was a dangerous man; I cautioned my friends to be careful. But, heady with triumph, still caught up in their mischievous roles, they ran down from the stage and danced before the courtiers' table.

" 'I am the author,' said my friend Salvatore, reaching forward to tweak the Duke's beard.

" 'No, I am the author!' insisted Giovanni, poking the nobleman in the ribs.

" 'I am! I am!' cried Claudio, screwing up his face and feigning a childish tantrum.

" 'Take these idiots and break their necks!' screamed the Doge of Venice, crashing his gigantic forearm against the plates and goblets. 'I will not have my dignity insulted this way!'

"I stood back, my feet rooted to the stage. Had I not been a fellow of such boundless courage, my heart would have stopped. Gradually, I realized that the Duke had not included me among the condemned. But, at the same time, I understood that there was nothing I could do to help my friends.

"The next morning, I watched them hanged in the courtyard, as a lesson for seditious actors. Clustered on the balconies, the Duke's guests watched, grinning uneasily, trying to understand if it was all still part of the previous evening's entertainment."

That is how you always ended the story, Flaminio, with that same description of the guests. "But what then?" I wanted to ask you. "What happened next? What happened when you left the palace?"

And this is what I think: I think you left the Doge's hall a determined man, Captain, the leader of a troupe, an adult with no more patience for the wildness of half-grown boys. Already, you had decided to gather together a group of actors who could perform perfectly under your direction, who could improvise faultlessly, who could fill the stage with complete, complex figures from life, unlike the mean, flat caricatures which had once delighted you and your friends from the seminary.

Naturally, it took some time to assemble such a group. You stole actors from other companies, interviewed shopgirls and magicians, recruited beggars from the gutters. But still, you were extremely selective about the men and women you chose for the permanent troupe, and all that picking and discarding took many, many years. By the time you saved me from the convent, many of you had been together a decade; and that was long before we had even seen Isabella Andreini!

But gradually, as I came to realize the exceedingly strange way in which you had chosen us, I wondered that it had not taken you forever.

You had typecast us perfectly, Captain. On the day I finally understood, I laughed out loud. It seemed absurd, impossible, and yet you had done it. You had found a group of actors so similar to the roles they played on stage that improvisation was effortless—they simply played themselves. And if, for the purposes of comedy, they agreed to exaggerate some aspect of their nature into a monstrous grotesque? The audience perceived the terrible self-doubt beneath Dottore's pompous display, and came away from your plays with a sense of having seen to the core of life.

Of course, you made your mistakes. We all know how Francesco fooled you again and again; who can say what tricks Isabella played? And how could you have known how many of us would come to resent you for refusing to acknowledge those private aspects of our souls, which we did not parade on stage? Yet, like all of your schemes, this one worked admirably: The Glorious Ones were a magnificent success.

But once in a while, Flaminio, I am tempted to think that

your plan for The Glorious Ones worked no better than your decision to entertain the Doge. I wonder if you did not introduce a poison into our blood, which has only begun to strangle our hearts. And, most of all, I ask myself whether that old scheme of yours will not prevent me from fulfilling your last wish, from compiling the true, factual history which you so desire.

For how can I begin to tell the truth, Flaminio, when the truth is that I myself was never quite sure just when we were acting?

II • BRIGHELLA

THAT CRAZY DWARF is petrified of dying, that coward. That's why she's always on my back, nagging me, breathing her nauseating stench down my neck.

"Brighella! Remember this? Remember that? Write it, write it, put it down in black and white."

"Go stick it up your ass," I tell her. "You're just out to keep your name alive after the worms start crawling through your rotten bones!"

"No," she says, with that proud, silly smile which makes me want to smack her. "It has nothing to do with me. Flaminio's ghost commanded it, in a dream."

"Fat chance," I say. "What self-respecting ghost would waste its time in the bedroom of a greasy toad like you? No, my dear, I know a coward when I see one. Remember how you were that night we slept together, always peeking out of the corner of your eye, terrified I'd roll you off the bed and crack your skull?"

"So you're the expert on cowards, Brighella?" she spits at me, her voice crackling with hatred.

"Indeed I am," I nod. "God knows, I've had plenty of practice. This whole troupe's as yellow as a cesspool, every one of those pissants but me and Isabella Andreini. And lately, watching her make moon-eyes at that big cow Pietro, I've even had my doubts about her. But there is no doubt in my mind that you are the most spineless of all, my slimy little jellyfish."

"*You're* the coward!" cries Armanda Ragusa, provoked to the edge of tears.

"Armanda," I say, "that remark is so witless—even for you—that I'm quite satisfied of having won our discussion."

Ladies and gentlemen of the future. I know what's running through your dim little brains. "Of course," you're thinking, "that Brighella had good reason to be so cocky. He was the one all the artists painted, he knew *his* immortality was secure. He knew that history would remember his nasty face, his wicked grin, his cold, vicious eyes. He knew everyone would see his short, skinny body, hunched up, crouched, ready to dart about like the gadfly he was.

Ah, my unborn audiences, you're no geniuses. Those fourth-rate scribblings have nothing to do with my fearlessness, nothing whatsoever! What kind of idiot do you think I am? What good would eternal fame do me if I were frying in the fires of hell?

No, my dull-witted friends, the reason I'm so brave is this: I know I'll never go to hell. I know my soul will never die. Because I, Brighella, the Gadfly, I alone have been absolutely promised eternal life!

You're wondering where I get the nerve to make such claims? I will tell you. I've had a vision, a real vision of holy salvation. Now, you want to know what it is. I've got your curiosity aroused. Your tongues are hanging out, you're covering yourselves with drool.

All right then. Since you're so eager, I'll tell it specially, just for you. But it's a long story, my friends—deeper and more complicated than anything your mean little spirits could comprehend. So I'll spare you the details, and make it short.

I was born into a family of petty crooks—gangsters, swindlers, whores, pimps, thieves. At the age of eighteen, I was caught with my hand in another man's pocket, and sentenced to be hanged from the gallows.

They marched me up to the scaffolding. They placed the noose around my neck, some idiot priest mumbled the prayers, the floor dropped out from under me.

And then, just at the right moment, the rope snapped. "What a pleasant surprise," I thought, as I tumbled gracefully through the air.

But suddenly, in those few brief moments before I landed nimbly on my feet, I heard the voice of God.

"The accused," said the Lord, "has been sentenced to Eternal Life!"

Of course I knew it was God. His tone was so shrill, so earsplitting, I had no doubt. My heart beat fast, relief washed through me, the air was singing in my ears.

Nevertheless, I managed to stand up straight and brush myself off; then, I bowed, and left the jail, a free man.

Since then, ladies and gentlemen, Brighella the Gadfly has never felt a moment's fear. I wasn't even ruffled that night I first met Flaminio Scala, that night I first stung him, in the tavern.

It had been years since my brush with death. I was back to my old ways, my old tricks. I spent my evenings in the cafés, picking fights with wealthy-looking drunks, and challenging them to step outside for a duel. Then my friends, who were hiding in a nearby alley, would jump out, steal the drunk's money, and run off.

One night, in Bergamo, I picked Flaminio Scala as my victim. It was a chancy bet; I couldn't really tell if he had money or not. But, judging from the way he was dressed, I assumed he was some kind of rich queer, the black sheep son of some wealthy family.

So I leaned towards him, jabbing my elbow into his ribs. "Hey," I said, "where'd you get such beautiful long hair?"

"From my head," muttered Flaminio, intent on his drink.

"Witty," I said. "Very witty, for such a drunk. Now tell me, did you borrow those fancy clothes from your sister?"

"No," he said, turning away.

"Faggot!" I hissed at him, as nastily as I could.

Suddenly, Flaminio Scala sat up very straight, and threw his wine in my face. "How dare you call me that!" he cried. "Don't you know who I am? I am Flaminio Scala, the most virile man in all Italy!"

"Let's discuss it outside," I said, looking towards the door.

"Nonsense!" shouted Flaminio. "We'll discuss it right here!" With that, he jumped up on the table, drew his sabre, and flourished, it in a figure eight. Then, he jumped down, and began to chase me around the tavern.

He chased me around the room, over the bar, throwing chairs, overturning tables. His swordsmanship was dazzling; even I, a criminal, was impressed. For I noticed that beneath his charade of fierceness and rage, he was moving carefully, like a dancer; he never touched me with the point of his sword.

At last, Flaminio cornered me, threw me down, and pinned me to the floor with his sabre.

"Brighella!" he cried. "Our gadfly! You are perfect!"

It had been a hair-raising scene. For years afterward, those cowardly barflies of Bergamo would talk about their night of terror in the tavern.

But I, Brighella, was not afraid. Right in the thick of it, I wasn't even ruffled.

No, ladies and gentlemen, I've never been frightened. Yet now, as I think back on my miserable career, I do recall a few nervous twitches, during that first trip to France.

Things were bad in those days, and it was all Flaminio's doing—Flaminio, with his constant cursing and carrying on, blaspheming, speaking of the Virgin Mary's body as if it were some hunk of mutton slung up on the butcher's hook.

"You loud-mouthed idiot!" I'd yell at him. "What's wrong with you? Don't you know that even God can only stand so much? You'll bring it down on all our heads, wait and see. I'd like to hear you talk like that when you're roasting in hell!"

But the fact was we were already in hell. That French trip was a disaster. Right from the start, I knew it would turn out that way. All those delays, those false starts, every day another letter from the king: "Hurry to Blois—don't bother—the nobles are assembled—no one is here—come in April—in August—September—November."

It was January by the time we left. We hardly had to spur our horses—that cold wind whipped us across France like a fleet of crippled sailboats. We traveled slowly, losing our way in blinding snowstorms, breaking our necks on the ice.

I rode last in line, complaining constantly. "Flaminio!" I whined. "This trip will be a catastrophe, mark my words. We're wasting our talents on those French jackasses! They'll drive us back across the border with feathers burning in our tails! We should have stayed home, playing the street fairs and carnivals. At least, we were making a decent living!"

But the Captain's ears were stuffed with delusions. All he could hear was his own fantasy of fame, immortality, great art! Ambition had sunk its fangs deep in him; its poison was making him a slavedriver. He made us rehearse all night, singing and dancing like madmen, even when we'd been traveling all day. Even when he let us go, we couldn't sleep; then he'd begin that infernal hammering, as he constructed those outrageous sets to impress the French king.

All that time I was the only one brave enough to complain, the only one sensible enough to resist Flaminio's madness. And, when that business with the Huguenots began, I was the only one who came right out and said what was on his mind.

It was the last week of the trip. We were so close to Blois, so near silken sheets, warm women, good wine—even I felt almost cheerful. Of course, the disaster had to happen then; we were off guard, we'd stopped expecting the worst.

One morning, as we stumbled along the icy road, a gang of grim-looking soldiers suddenly swooped down on us from beyond a bend. Shouting and waving their swords, they galloped towards us, bearing down hard, until they were so near that I could see the foam from their horses freezing in the cold air.

"Fight to the death!" I shrieked. "Fight to the death!" For, though I knew that a handful of puny actors had no chance against those shiny sabres, I couldn't resist the temptation to make the others feel worse.

Within minutes our enemies had surrounded us. Their leader seized the bridle of Flaminio's horse, and led us across the meadow. Those cowardly actors were quiet as mice; Columbina and Vittoria sniveled with terror. I grinned devilishly at one of our captors, but the smile soon died on my lips. I'd never seen such hatred on anyone's face, not even among the poor suckers I'd swindled as a boy.

At last, we found ourselves in a drafty cave, heated by one pathetic, smoking log. A dozen sentries guarded the entrance, trying hard not to peek inside. Just beyond them, Flaminio Scala was trying in his worthless schoolboy French, to negotiate with their commander.

By the time he joined us inside, the Captain's face was the same color as the dirty snow.

"Who are they?" demanded Vittoria, strutting and ruffling her feathers like a fat turkey. "What do they want?"

"They're Protestants," spat Flaminio, as if he'd suddenly become the great defender of the faith.

"Do they want us to perform for *them*?" asked Vittoria.

"They want us to do our most gruesome death scenes," replied Flaminio. "They want our heads to go on tour, at the ends of pikes, as a little morality play about their country's decadence."

It was then that The Glorious Ones went crazy with fear. That cowardly Jew Pantalone sat alone in a far corner of the cave, hugging himself and shivering. The Doctor kept rushing towards the mouth of the cavern, scanning the sky and insisting that it was essential for his research to know the exact position of the sun. And Vittoria paraded back and forth, making a great show of indignation, flashing her breasts at our jailers as if the mere sight of that pimply flesh would turn the Huguenots into panting adolescents.

If Isabella had been there, we'd have been free in an instant. She'd have bewitched those guards, had them talking about their wives and children; she'd have serenaded them with poetry so sweet that the tears would have blinded their eyes. But Vittoria was the lady of the troupe then. It was a different story. All she did was make everyone sick.'

At last, I lost patience with the whole situation. "Hey!" I shouted, poking Francesco Andreini. "Look at that Captain of ours over there! Instead of getting us out of this mess, he's quaking in his boots, because Vittoria's being mean to him. Why not take over, Andreini, and keep us from rotting in here like rats in a trap? That feeble old man's unfit to be our leader!"

Andreini looked at the Captain, then back at me. "Flaminio is not yet thirty," he replied, in that confident, maddening way of his. "He's hardly what you might call feeble. I'm still willing to trust him."

That's the kind of bastard Francesco Andreini was! He left me standing there, looking bad, dirty-handed, the only traitor in the loyal band. But he knew I was right—not five minutes later, he walked quietly towards the entrance, and beckoned to the Huguenot leader.

From inside the cave, we watched Andreini, drooping over

the Frenchman. Francesco was skinny as a rail in those days; beneath that halo of light, curly hair, he looked like a sunflower. He argued for almost an hour, gesturing, like a natural-born Frenchman, with those long, spidery hands.

At last, the commander nodded, and Francesco reentered the cave. And at that moment, when I saw the hot look Vittoria gave him, I knew that Francesco Andreini had begun to direct another nasty little drama.

Flaminio, too, saw that look on her face. "What happened?" he asked, playing that cowardly role which came to him so naturally.

"In three days," Andreini replied, "we will be free."

"Dead or alive?" asked the Captain.

"Exactly," snapped Francesco. "Dead or alive."

After a brief pause, he continued. "I have persuaded the Huguenots that their interests might be better served if they allowed the French king to ransom us for a small fortune. They have sent a courier to Blois. And, in seventy-two hours, we will learn of the royal decision."

"You're not so clever, Andreini," I shouted, enraged by the smugness on his big moon-face. "You just know how to reach that greedy pig hidden inside of everyone."

Francesco only smiled at me, in a way which made me want to strangle him. Then, he sat down to wait.

And, for the first time, we followed his lead. Sitting and sleeping on the cold ground, we waited out the long three days. What else was there to do?

All that time, Francesco Andreini remained calm. He never grew restless, no matter how loudly those cowardly actors whimpered and moaned—nor did he move a muscle at the end, when the sight of that messenger riding up with twenty sacks of gold made those fools jump up and crack their skulls against the roof of the cave.

Andreini's calmness surprised me; I'd thought *I* was the only brave one in the bunch. But, as we gathered our things and prepared to leave the cave, Andreini did something which surprised me even more.

"Wait!" he cried, blocking the entrance with his long arms. "Perhaps Brighella was right. Perhaps I should be the one to take the first steps out of here."

We froze in our tracks; our mouths hung open. In those days, we never imagined that Andreini would seriously consider such a thing. Even when I'd suggested it, I'd been joking; I didn't mean it.

Flaminio was facing outwards, towards the light. He straightened his shoulders, and, without turning around, began to speak.

"If you still intend to perform before the King of France next week," he said, "I suggest that you remain beneath the leadership of the most talented actor, director, stagehand, musician, and singer among you. Unless you desire to disgrace yourselves before royalty, I suggest that you stay beneath the brilliant command of Flaminio Seal a, leader of The Glorious Ones."

That coward Andreini bowed his head, and motioned for us to precede him from the cave. But, as I brushed past him, I looked into his eyes, and realized that the drama he'd begun in that cave was not yet over.

Two days later, we were perfumed so sweetly that we couldn't have offended a single hair in the French king's snotty nostril. No one could have told that we'd just spent all that time encrusted with shit and mud. We sparkled like angels dropped in from heaven—and that was exactly what those French aborigines thought we were!

God, what jackasses they made of themselves, banging their goblets against the table and screaming. I couldn't find a joke too dirty for them; I couldn't play a prank too nasty for their refined tastes. They were at us all the time, those filthy lechers— refilling the women's wineglasses, patting their backsides. Their wives bent over backwards, luring us up to their rooms. Even the king was in on it—trying to peer down Vittoria's bodice, getting eyestrain; you'd have thought they were the only breasts in all France. And how could I forget those senile old retainers who crowded around us, those doddering half-wits who asked if our stage effects were in fact great feats of magic?

Feats of magic! Those were the geniuses of the French court! No wonder the country was in such bad shape!

Still, I must admit: Flaminio outdid himself that week we spent at Blois. All those fancy devices he invented—the dancing moon, the raging flood, the flying lovers. I sweated blood, pulling the ropes on those pasteboard pirate galleons!

He himself was always strutting like a gander, declaiming like an arrogant fool. He exaggerated all the worst aspects of the Captain's part. His boastful leadership was so outrageous that, by comparison, the French king seemed as wise and prudent a monarch as the Lord Himself.

The courtiers loved it. And each day Flaminio grew fatter, more bloated with success and pride, until we took to calling him "The Pope."

The Pope! Some joke! We had no idea what we were saying, we should have knocked on wood! Because, on the eighth day of our stay, the real thing showed up!

He called himself the Cardinal, the Monseigneur—who can keep track of the fancy names those French monks take on? He was a thin, balding, ugly fellow; he minced and pranced like a billy goat on his way across the room. But, as he moved towards the king, each tap of his high heels sounded like the crack of doom.

Right then, I knew the whole story. It was a feeling I remembered from the old days, when I was always on the run: someone enters the room, and you know that there's trouble, and the trouble means you.

"Flaminio Scala!" I hissed. "This play is just about over!"

Just as I'd predicted, the Cardinal leaned down, and whispered in the king's ear. The king's dumb face twitched with confusion. Then, he rose and followed the priest out the door.

A moment later, the king returned, grinning sheepishly. "Tonight," he said, pointing towards the door.

"You mean we should discontinue our performance until tonight?" asked the Captain.

"I mean you should leave my court tonight," replied the king, with a silly, helpless shrug. "The Church of France disapproves of the theater in general, of your lewdness in particular. Therefore, you are expected to be on the other side of the border within ten days."

"My beloved Sovereign!" cried Flaminio, racing towards the throne. "I cannot believe that the most equitable and enlightened ruler in all Christendom could do us such a grave injustice! We meant no harm, I assure you. We were only trying to please. And I was actually under the impression—correct me, my lord, if I am wrong—that we had managed to amuse you.

"Why, then, should a leader of your boundless generosity reward us so poorly? Is it possible that our good-natured vulgarity has offended the spotless purity of your ladies? Were our songs too loud for you, our dances too sensual, our jokes too coarse? If so, I. apologize, Your Majesty. And, from the depths of my contrition, I implore you to consider our humble and inconvenient position.

"It will require at least five days for us to gather together our equipment. And it was my dearest hope—surely this cannot disturb your pious and holy churchmen—that you Would allow us to perform for several weeks in the towns and cities of your glorious land, so that we might gain a few extra pennies to help defray the costs of our journey."

After five minutes of this disgusting display, even Flaminio realized that the king wasn't listening. The Captain turned his back on the throne, and walked towards the door. His eyes were downcast. As he passed the stage, he couldn't look at us. I cleared my throat and spat, right in his path. But an ocean of my spit couldn't have conveyed half the contempt on Francesco Andreini's face.

FRANCINE PROSE

Needless to say, the journey home made the trip out seem sweeter than crossing the Jordan. No one smiled, no one laughed, no one even talked except Vittoria, who harangued the Captain mercilessly. During the day, Flaminio stared straight ahead; as soon as we reached the inns, he rushed off to bed. The Captain still rode in front, but Andreini had moved to the very back; riding between them, the rest of us almost choked on the thickness in the air.

Poor crazy Flaminio! Even I almost pitied him. "He's finished now," I thought. "His job is free for the asking. These actors would follow Peter the Hermit, if he came along preaching another crusade."

But late one night, at an inn just south of Turin, something happened which made me suspect that the old lunatic still had a few clever tricks up his sleeve.

It was after a dinner of foul, greasy broth. We were all grumpy, waiting to digest that slop so we could go to bed. That evening, for the first time since Blois, Flaminio didn't go straight to sleep. Instead, he walked over to the fireplace, then wheeled around to face us.

"My dearest Glorious Ones," he began. "It is my proposal that we return to Venice. And there, amid the comforts of that lovely city, we shall decide the future of our troupe. But, before that, I would like to give one last performance, tomorrow morning, at a spot not far from here."

"Why, Captain?" shouted Vittoria. "So you can kiss the ass of one last nobleman?"

The Captain threw her an accusing look. "There will be no noblemen in the audience," he replied. "I would like us to perform before a crowd of poor, deprived innocents, at the local convent orphanage."

It took me two seconds to figure out what that filthy blasphemer had in mind. "Flaminio!" I cried. "You're like an open casket. We can see inside you, straight to all the rot and putre-

32

faction in your soul. I understand your plan perfectly. You'll do anything to revenge yourself on the church. You'll corrupt babies, molest little children, scandalize a convent full of blameless nuns. That's your idea, isn't it—to pay back those pious friars, to make yourself our hero, our avenger, the upholder of our honor?"

"Not at all," he replied. "I have no more interest in being your hero, or even your leader. The only thing which concerns me now is the prospect of making my peace with God. I have suddenly come to understand why He has cursed me so cruelly, why my luck has grown so bad. For, if each of my sins were a single grain of sand, the Sahara would seem like a narrow shoal compared to the vast desert which would separate me from the Blessed Lord.

"And now, I am hoping that this small act of piety, *this* pitiful performance in the name of charity, will persuade Him to turn His face towards me across the burning wasteland."

"Don't flatter yourself, Captain," muttered Vittoria. "Only in your wildest dreams have you sinned so often."

Ah, Vittoria. At moments like that, I almost liked her. For a moment, Flaminio's eyes narrowed with cowardice. Then, they widened again, and began to glow with a peculiar light.

"What kind of man do you think I am?" he cried. "What good would it do me to be known as a great sinner? Why should I want that? Don't you realize how serious I am, how I'd do anything on earth for a clear conscience, how desperately I hunger for spiritual peace?"

"The only thing you hunger for is Vittoria's ass!" I shouted.

But I was the only one speaking. The others had fallen silent; and, as I followed their bug-eyed stares, I saw what had made them so quiet.

Even with my razor-sharp wit, I can hardly describe or explain it. But after it was over, and we discussed it, the actors agreed that we'd all seen the same thing:

The bright lights came on in Flaminio's eyes, as if they were a theater. And there, on the stage inside those gleaming discs, we saw the Play of the Prodigal Son, with Flaminio Scala in the title role. We saw him squander his father's money, break his mother's heart. We saw him traveling, gambling, whoring, drinking, smoking opium. We saw the anguish which tortured him near the end, and the sweet smile of contentment which came over his face when at last his father pardoned him. And we heard the words of the Bible, "Forgive, that you may be forgiven."

To this day, I don't know if Flaminio Scala bewitched us that night, or if it was actually another miracle in my long career of wonders. But those other dimwits weren't so concerned with fine spiritual distinctions.

By the time Flaminio went off to bed, he was their leader again. He'd reconquered them with the power of his vision. They were overjoyed, those idiots—delighted that everything was neat and tidy. Now, they'd never have to think for themselves. Even Andreini looked relieved.

The subsequent trip to the convent was so cheerful, it almost made me vomit. And there, when those sentimental fools saw their own stupid tricks bring such happiness to the orphans, they were as pleased as if they'd gone straight to Paradise.

But I was the only one who wasn't fooled. All the while, I sulked and fretted, trying to figure out what was in the Captain's mind.

I am as sharp and crafty as a gadfly, ladies and gentlemen. Still, when I reach heaven, I pray that the Lord will not give me the job of judge at the pearly gates. For even I, Brighella, the only one of The Glorious Ones with firsthand knowledge of holy things—even I have never been sure if Flaminio's repentance was sincere. If he was just pretending, if it was all a plot to regain the company's favor, then how did he make us see that vision? And what possible reason could he have had for adopting that repulsive little dwarf, if not as a act of charity and devotion?

Through the years, I've asked myself those questions many times. But I know there's only one way I'll ever discover the truth.

When the Lord finally keeps his promise, and I'm admitted into heaven, I'll look all around me for Flaminio's soul. And, if he isn't there, if I can't find him in any of the golden dwellings and lush gardens, men I'll know that Flaminio Scala, the leader of The Glorious Ones, was a far better actor than I thought.

III • PANTALONE

"IF YOU REALLY WANT SOMETHING DONE," my mother used to say, "ask a woman who loves you to do it." She was talking about herself, of course—but was she also making a prediction? Is that why I've never gotten anything done in my life, mother? Because I've never found a woman who loved me?

"Don't kill yourself with self-pity," I can hear her saying. And she's right. But sometimes I can't help it—lately, it's been pricking me like a big thorn in the seat of my pants. Even poor Flaminio, I think, even poor Flaminio wound up one step ahead of me. Armanda Ragusa's no bargain, I'll admit—but the devotion of that pitiful thing is better than anything I've ever gotten. Now, as I watch her bustling among the actors, doing Flaminio's bidding as radiantly as if it were Jesus Christ Himself who'd visited her in that dream, I choke with envy. If I want my memorial prayers chanted, I'll have to sing them myself.

Perhaps I should never have expected more. I should have known better. I was no longer a boy when I joined the troupe. Already I'd worked twenty years as a tailor, and as my mother's nurse.

Day after day, I'd stitch until my fingers bled; I'd run straight home to feed her tea with lemon until she fell asleep. And, late at night, as I thought about the miserable life I was leading, I began to realize what sort of man I was.

A kindlier person would have called me a student of human nature. But I wasn't so kind to myself, I knew the truth.

I was the stranger, the observer, the spy, the one who stands outside of life, looking in. I was the sort of man whom others fear; because, watching from such a great distance, I could often see straight to the heart of people, and guess the secrets which they'd rather keep hidden.

It was true. Sometimes, I could read a customer's mind so well that I could cut a coat to fit his most secret desires. But sometimes I was wrong.

I was wrong, for example, about Flaminio Scala. That first time he charged into my store, demanding a length of pink lace for a woman's stockings, I misread him. I took one look at his broad shoulders, his healthy beard, his ruddy cheeks, and hated him on sight.

"This one moves right through the middle of life," I thought. "This one has all the adventures, fights the ladies off his back, catches those showers of gold coins."

I hated him so much I wanted to humiliate him, I wanted to rob him blind. And it was only my fear of him which kept me from cheating him more than I did.

Still, he noticed the slight—shall we say—discrepancy in our transaction. As I watched him counting and recounting his change, the needle trembled in my fingers, and I waited for his big, strong hand to reach out and grab me.

But I was misreading him again. Much to my surprise, he began to grin. He looked me up and down, gazing at my hooked nose, my pale skin, my stooped, thin body. He stared at the tufts of reddish hair which stuck out from beneath my skullcap like the feathers of a duck.

"Pantalone!" he cried at last. "My crabby old Jew!"

I had no idea what he meant. Nevertheless, I took it from him, just as I wound up taking it from all of them.

"What do you mean?" I asked, in a voice intended to be cold and haughty.

"I mean you shall travel with my acting troupe and be Pantalone," explained Flaminio. "You will play the miserly Jew, the cuckold, the betrayed father, the old schemer whom everyone tries to mock and fool. You'll lead the life of a great artist, my dear fellow. You'll see the seven wonders of the world. You'll win untold fortune, fame, glory. Women will throw themselves at your feet. Think it over. Tell me your decision tomorrow; I'll be back at noon."

After he left, my head was spinning. My mother had just died, so I was free to go with him. But I couldn't make up my mind. On the one hand, my heart was full of doubt. I was afraid to leave my comfortable home, and I knew what abuse I'd be taking in that role, in that insult to myself and my race. On the other hand, I had visions—dreams of changing my life, of breaking through to the center of things, of finding thrilling excitement and wild love. And that seed of vanity which the Captain had planted in my soul had already begun to spread like a cancer.

So I shook my head: yes. I sold my store, and went with him.

As always, I should have listened to my doubts. They were the only things which never misled me. I missed my secure position in the shop. I got all the abuse I'd expected, and more. Led by that vicious Brighella, they taunted me constantly, joking about my religion, my appearance, my so-called stinginess, my obsession with money. And it was all because of what I was— the outsider, the watcher. I knew what was going on inside their hearts, and it made them uneasy.

As a matter of fact, I was no more obsessed with money than the rest of them. So what, if I was the only one who saw all that trouble with the church in terms of gold and silver? It wasn't *my* church; I was the only one who didn't feel that secret thrill of terror in his soul.

But, knowing how sensitive I was, they loved to torture me about it; they went out of their way to find new excuses to hurt me. That was why they made me the treasurer.

"Pantalone will be good at the job," said Flaminio Scala one night, after a long day of drinking. "He is an expert at hoarding his own money. Surely, he can be trusted with ours."

The others laughed uproariously. They were bored with each other again—there was nothing to do but pick on me. So they held a general election, and I was appointed to carry the cashbox, to keep the accounts, to divide the money, and settle the wrangling which went on as those dogs all scrambled after the same pitiful bones. It was also my job to foil them in their constant attempts to cheat me of my rightful portion; it was just as we played it on stage.

As it happened, I *was* good at the job. And, though they called me a greedy usurer, a lying cheat, a thieving Jew—still, my word was often the only thing which kept them from killing each other over pennies. I was good at it, all right, but not for the reasons they thought. It wasn't that I was born with a talent for finance in my blood, with a neat stack of coins for a heart, with eyes that added and subtracted like wondrous machines.

No, the reason I handled the money so well was this: the money was all I had. It was my only raft in that vast sea of disappointment.

I hadn't gotten any of the other things I'd hoped to find in Flaminio's troupe. I hadn't moved any closer to the heart of life. I was still the outsider, watching the others as if a needle and thread were always passing between us.

I'd wanted thrilling adventure; I'd gotten nothing but the great pleasure of being kidnapped, scared to death, almost massacred. I'd dreamed of wild love, but there was none of that for me. I suppose I could have had Armanda for the asking, and Columbina with a little effort, or any of those little girls who flocked to our tents after the shows. But that wasn't what I wanted. Were I forty years younger, I might be persuaded to take on that Isabella; but there's no chance of that on this earth. And on those rare occasions when I did meet a lady who appealed to me—a mature actress from another troupe, perhaps—something about me always seemed to drive her away. Maybe it was the fact that I was no longer a young man; I was foolish to have expected more.

Of course, it was love of a kind I got from Vittoria, but it wasn't the kind I'd imagined. After those first times I played Pantalone to her Inamorata, she began to treat me as she did in the scenarios—as the old man, the trusted uncle. When she wasn't too busy with her lovers, she'd often confide in me. I resented it, going straight from the role of the son to that of the father, with nothing in between; I'd wanted something else. And the truth was: I didn't really *like* Vittoria and her coarse ways. I despised her when she joined the others in mocking me.

But I took what I could get. And so, for many years, I listened to Vittoria tell me the story of that strange struggle between Francesco and the Captain. I heard her version; but of course, I could have guessed those secrets just as well on my own.

She was right in the midst of it—my dumb, fat, loud, arrogant daughter. They tossed her around like a bean-bag, those two. She was nothing but a pawn to them; I told her so a million times.

"Don't play the know-it-all old man with me," she'd snap. "I'm a grown woman. I can take care of myself."

But I knew better, because I knew she hadn't been a grown woman when it started.

"I was seventeen then," she told me once. "I was a pretty girl, though by no means the prettiest in town, and I knew it. To make matters worse, my family was poor, there was nothing in my dowry. For those reasons, I was still single, though most of my friends had been married for years. I was desperate, Pantalone, believe me—I was so curious, so eager to lose my virginity.

"So when Flaminio and his worthless friends came to play in our city, they seemed like a good prospect. They were young, handsome enough; most important, they were strangers, who wouldn't stick around to ruin my reputation.

"I took to haunting the marketplace whenever they performed. I picked out Flaminio as the easiest target, then mooned at him constantly with my big eyes. I'd lounge against the pillars in the plaza, my breasts stuck out, grinning at Flaminio with what I hoped was a wanton look.

And finally, late one night, I got up my nerve and went to his room at the inn. Flaminio, Brighella, and Thomasso—who was still with the troupe then—were seated on the bed, staring into space, passing around a huge flask of wine. They were startled by my knock; they gazed blankly at me as I entered the room.

"I've come," I stammered, forcing a big, brazen grin, "because I so much admire your acting."

"Do you admire it enough to take on all three of us at once?" asked that pig Brighella, thrusting at me with his hips.

Now, of course, I'd know enough to slap his face for such a remark. But you wouldn't have recognized me then, Pantalone. I was so innocent, I wasn't prepared. All I could do was look down at the ground.

"I can see we have ourselves a lady here," said Thomasso, who always fancied himself a great gentleman. "Perhaps we should retire, Brighella, and leave Flaminio with his guest."

"And that was how I spent my first night of love," said Vittoria, spitting on the ground as she pronounced the word. "The next morning, I woke up and realized what I'd done.

" 'No one will every marry me now,' I thought. 'I've given up all my chances for this dumb sonofabitch Flaminio Scala.'

I began to weep big gushes of tears, until Flaminio couldn't stand it any more.

"Get out of here," he barked. "No one asked you to come, anyway."

But, as my sobbing grew louder, he began to sweat a little; he was worried that I'd wake the neighbors, have him run out of town. "My dearest young lady," he said, all sweetness and light. "Nothing terrible has happened, I assure you. Everything will be all right, you'll see."

"It won't!" I cried. "I've destroyed myself, disgraced my family. I can't stay in this city any more. Take me with you, I beg you. Let me travel with your troupe. Don't leave me here to face the shame."

"I'm sorry," he said, trying to look sincere. "Although you are certainly the most loveable young woman who has ever graced my bedroom, I regret to say that there is no way."

"But I'll kill myself," I moaned. "I'll go to hell, and reach up to drag you down with me."

For a moment, Flaminio hesitated; then, he grew stern again. "That is your decision," he said.

So I decided to try another tack. "Listen!" I cried. "I love you! I want to be with you! I'll do anything, go anywhere. I'll shine your boots, walk naked on the stage if you ask me. But I can't stand the thought of being separated from you, even for an instant!"

Flaminio stared at me for a long time, knitting his brows in that ugly way he does when he's thinking. "Perhaps our troupe *could* use a woman," he said at last. "Our scenarios might take on another dimension. You could play the Inamorata, the girl half-crazy with love. I'd play Amante, your suitor. You could worship me and sing my praises to your heart's content. The ladies in our audience will go wild over it; and their husbands will love to watch your breasts bounce and jiggle as you run across the stage in a lovesick frenzy."

"That was my gallant invitation to join The Glorious Ones,"

sneered Vittoria. "And, if I'd only listened well, I'd have known how that bastard Flaminio was going to treat me. I'd have stayed home, even if it had meant going into a convent.

"Oh, he was disgusting to me in those days. He acted like I was his footstool, kicked me around like some piece of garbage from the gutter. 'Vittoria,' he'd say, 'get my cloak! I could teach a dog to fetch better than you! Vittoria, wash my hose. It's the only job you're suited for.' "

"Why did you put up with it?" I asked her. "Did you love him?"

"Love him?!" she replied. "Love that filthy pig Flaminio Scala?! Love him always jumping on me like I was a horse, riding me, in and out, in and out, off before I even knew what was happening?! That's not love, that's not the kind of thing that wins a woman's heart. And I only let him keep on doing *that* until I was old enough to stand up for myself!

"No, I only took it because I had no choice. I knew that if I left the troupe, I'd have to work on my back, being ridden by more men than one. That was why I fetched Flaminio's cloak— because the money for my supper was in his pockets!"

But I think Vittoria was fooling herself—unless, poor thing, she'd managed to forget the truth. Because I think she did love Flaminio once, with that peculiar love which women always have for their first man. And that old love was part of the web she fell into, that web Francesco and Flaminio wove around each other like maddened spiders.

For, if she never loved him, how could she have come to hate him so much?

"One morning," she told me, "I woke up and decided I'd had enough. That afternoon, on stage, I listened very carefully to the applause I got; and suddenly I realized that Flaminio *needed* the Inamorata, the lovesick young girl. The audiences loved her like their own daughters, their sisters, themselves at an earlier age. They were so attached to her, they'd *kill* Flaminio if he tried to play their towns without the Inamorata.

FRANCINE PROSE

"At that moment, I knew I was free. 'Flaminio,' I said, the next time he came to my bed, 'go jerk off.'

"From that day on, I couldn't stand the sight of Flaminio Scala. I couldn't stand talking to him, or even being in the same room with him. It wasn't some game I was playing to win his affection—believe me, it was the real thing. I'd been freed from his power; everything about him made my flesh creep. I forbade him to come near my tent; whenever I saw him, it was all I could do to keep from vomiting.

"It was such a great change in me, Pantalone, it had to affect my acting. I couldn't even fake it anymore. I couldn't pretend to believe that the light in Flaminio's beady eyes was as sweet to me as the first burst of sun after a spring rain. How could I have said such a thing with a straight face? How could I have fooled the audience into thinking I meant it?

"So that's why the role of the Inamorata had to change. She could no longer toss on her bed, crying for her man. So he had to begin crying for her.

"But I wasn't as smart as I thought, Pantalone. If I'd been a little more experienced, I'd have known that it would end the way it did. I'd have known that creep Flaminio would fall madly in love with me, that he'd lose his mind and keep pestering me to this very day!"

I myself knew the rest of Vittoria's story. It had been like that ever since I joined the troupe. The Captain was making a fool of himself over Vittoria. It was high comedy. Everyone laughed about it—except, of course, for that poor dwarf, who had such a crush on him that she shut her eyes to the whole thing.

Sometimes, I think it was that madness for Vittoria which first lowered Flaminio's station in the eyes of the others. To tell the truth, I pitied him. I had sympathy for his dreams of glory, of wild love; I had a few of them myself. And I pitied him for being so obsessed with that worthless Vittoria. She had a good heart, I suppose, but she was so coarse, so graceless, so common-looking—I couldn't understand how any sensible man could worship her so passionately.

But no one could ever accuse Flaminio Scala of being a sensible man. He stubbornly insisted on playing the role of the Lover, as well as that of the Captain. Knowing what we knew, it was embarrassing to watch him perform. He grovelled on his knees, licked the dust off Vittoria's shoes, tried to put his hands all over her.

"Perhaps you underestimate me now," he'd sigh on stage. "But someday, when I am immortal, when I am enthroned with the gods in heaven, and all the nightingales on earth have learned to sing my name, *then* you will know what I was, *then* you will know what kind of man loved you!"

"When you are immortal," the Inamorata would giggle, "I'll be rotting in my grave."

But of course, it was Flaminio who wrote the plays; despite Vittoria's protests, the dramas ended the way *he* wanted. The hero was so noble that he *had* to win the girl. Nothing else seemed possible. The scenarios always ended with the two of them embracing, center stage.

The audiences loved it. Flaminio and Vittoria were a terrific success; their popularity filled my treasury. It was Amante and the Inamorata who got us invited to France.

But, after that miserable journey, after that incident in the cave and that disgrace at court, the roles of the Lover and his mistress began to change again.

It was obvious, I suppose. But, for a long time, no one noticed. They'd all been under Flaminio's spell since that dramatic repentance scene. Even I—Pantalone, the observer—even I failed to see how craftily Andreini was working. No one even suspected until that famous show at Perugia, when he pulled the rabbit out of his cap, for everyone to see.

He was always a sneaky one, Andreini. He calls himself a realist. But I call him a schemer, a conniver. If I was really the miser they say, you'd think I'd like Francesco; now that he and

Isabella are in charge, I need two boys to help me with the cashboxes. But I could never trust a man who has everything plotted out in advance, who knows every move, every turn. His brain is like a chessboard. There are lumps of ice in his heart. He moves slowly, sinuously, like a snake.

Of course, Andreini's changed since Isabella's started leading him down a few tricky paths of her own. But in those days, Francesco was a master. His scheme was so clever, so well executed, so perfectly obvious! On that night at Perugia, when we finally saw it, we were filled with admiration.

Who would have suspected? In the beginning, Andreini had been taken into the troupe to play Arlechino—the trickster, the clown, the half-wild cat, the cold eye. But, for the most part, he'd been hired for his acrobatics, his body.

According to Vittoria, he'd come up from the audience one day and astounded the entire company with an amazing display of gymnastics—somersaults, leaps, and contortions which he claimed to have learned among the Chinese and Turks.

Right then, Flaminio knew he'd discovered a gold mine. Usually, the acrobats were small, wiry fellows like Brighella. Flaminio realized that the crowds had never seen anything like Francesco before. When they saw his long-limbed body cartwheeling across the stage, they'd think they were watching some exotic, wild animal.

So for a long time, we thought of him as the athlete. Years passed before that sneaky Andreini let us know that he also spoke five languages, mimed like an angel, wrote like a professional. But, in those days, he and Flaminio were so close that the Captain seemed genuinely pleased to discover his friend's accomplishments. So he let Andreini play a bigger and bigger part.

And Francesco made a good Arlechino—somersaulting in the window, slinking around the edges of the stage, popping up from nowhere in the middle of the Lovers' most intimate dialogues. Dressed in that black and white patched suit, he shifted

THE GLORIOUS ONES

his weight back and forth from one foot to the other, holding long conversations with himself. He mocked the Lovers' passion, parodied their endearments, jeered at their troubles. He was always dragging the Inamorata off to stage right, to tell her she was wasting her time on a silly fool like Amante; then, he'd do the same to Flaminio, at stage left. He made the audiences laugh, but all his insults and nasty pranks only made them love the Lovers more.

And then, on that night in Perugia, everything changed.

It was a hot, damp August evening. The plaza was crowded with townspeople and university students. That night, the moment Arlechino jumped on stage, I knew that there was something peculiar about his style. A moment later, I realized what it was.

There was a double edge to his performance. Andreini was acting so brilliantly, he was managing to convey an odd sense about Arlechino. Suddenly, it was the clown who seemed to be the real lover. *He* was the one whose passion for Vittoria surpassed the brightness of the sun, the mystery of the Sphinx, the fierceness of the tiger. And all his mean remarks, all his cold, cruel joking, seemed intended as a tragic mask, to hide his true emotion.

That night, Andreini created a new Arlechino, a clown so eloquent, so passionate, so moving that he nearly broke *my* heart. I looked around to see if the audience realized what was happening, for it seemed that *they* couldn't fail to respond.

And I was right. Their eyes watered with sympathy every time Arlechino and Inamorata were alone on stage. But whenever the Lover appeared, their faces darkened, as if *he* were the intruder, the foil. As the play went on, and the lovesick clown drew no closer to his beloved, the mood of the crowd grew steadily uglier, more restless, until it began to make me uneasy.

The others felt it, too. "Watch out, Andreini!" hissed Brighella, interrupting the show. "Remember: these are sex-starved, drunken university students, who take these things seriously!"

But Andreini couldn't hear. He, Flaminio, and Vittoria were enmeshed in it together. And perhaps they would have remained entangled forever if that crazy riot hadn't broken out.

It was at the very end of the play. As always, Flaminio and Vittoria were embracing, center stage. But this time, Francesco stood in the wings, miming a remarkable show of noble suffering.

As soon as the audience realized that the drama was really over, that Arlechino would never win his love, a shocked silence fell over the crowd. Then, a storm of murmurs arose—whispers so hostile, so threatening, so unmistakable in their intent, that I knew enough to run for cover.

From the doorway of the inn, I watched the young men. Many of them were still in their academic gowns; yet they shouted, roared, grabbed rotten vegetables from the stores. They ripped up cobblestones from the plaza, and began to heave them at Flaminio.

"The woman belongs to Arlechino!" they yelled. They ran up on stage, grabbed the actors, and shook them like rugs. "Give the woman to Arlechino, or we'll hold you prisoner here until you rot!"

When at last Flaminio broke free of his captors, all the spirit had left his face. "All right, gentlemen," he said. "You are absolutely correct. There is a short epilogue to this drama, which we somehow forgot to perform. Return to your places, if you will, and prepare to watch the brilliant conclusion to our entertaining little show."

That last scene was so easy to improvise, a child could have done it. As the crowd moved back, Flaminio gave a short speech, acknowledging Arlechino as the true Lover, and admitting his error in having claimed the Inamorata's hand. Then, Francesco and Vittoria ran out from opposite wings, and met in a joyous embrace.

Cheering wildly, the students slapped each other's backs, and went home.

Andreini's trick had worked perfectly. From then on, he was the Lover, the star, the one whose eloquence drew such floods of sympathy from the crowd. There was no way for Flaminio to play Amante any more; he limited himself to the role of the Captain.

Indeed, he played the Captain more and more, onstage and off. He bragged like the admiral of a toy boat, raged like a frenzied bull. He was always berating Vittoria for having betrayed his love, always scolding Francesco for a million failures and inadequacies.

But poor dumb Vittoria, who could never see further than the coarse nose on her face, was delighted by the change.

"I like playing opposite Andreini," she told me. "He's so much more talented, more graceful. His kiss is so much sweeter than stinking Flaminio Scala's. He's so much easier to respond to, he's helping me, my acting is better than ever."

And it was true. But there was a familiar note in her voice, which I'd heard before, among the young brides who'd come into my shop to buy cloth for their husbands' suits. It was the way women talked about the men they loved.

As I listened to Vittoria, my head ached with envy. I knew no one would ever speak about me that way. "Vittoria," I said, "watch out for Andreini. He's a schemer. He's got his sights set on bigger game than you."

"Don't play the father with me, Pantalone," she said. "You'll only make me like him more."

And so my big cow of a daughter stumbled into Andreini's trap. Day after day, I watched him work his magic on her, courting her with stories and sweet, flowery speeches. And I watched her falling in love with him.

"Andreini doesn't care about you," I warned her. "Anyone in the troupe will tell you the same thing. It's just another one of his tricks. He's playing with you, using you; he's just doing it to make the Captain mad."

But women never listen to me; I'm not that sort of man. Vittoria continued in her foolishness, and, to tell the truth, she blossomed in it; the Inamorata was never sweeter. The audiences loved to see her trying every charm, every small grace, every ruse in her efforts to enchant Francesco. They showered her with wine-red roses and silver coins.

Often I stood offstage and wondered: does the audience know it's real? Is that why they like it so much? Do they know it's real when the Captain hurls himself across stage in clownish agony, begging the Inamorata to sleep with him?

Did they know it was real that night in Venice, when, in an unexpected improvisation, Vittoria suddenly changed the scenario, and consented to the Captain's pleas?

I knew. She came and told me so, the night it happened. "I told that old jackass Flaminio he can have me one more time," she said, pacing nervously back and forth. "I've invited him to come to my tent tonight. If *that* doesn't bring Andreini around, nothing will!"

"Why are you doing this?" I cried. "You're playing straight into Francesco's hands. You're helping him destroy the Captain! Is that what you want? Do you hate Flaminio so much? Don't you know better than to play Andreini's fool?"

Vittoria stared at me, her dull eyes brimming with sadness. Suddenly, I pitied her, because I knew that her love for Francesco was real.

"It's the only way," she said. "I'm desperate. He's got another woman, somewhere in the wealthy part of town. Everyone talks about it, it's common knowledge: he visits her once a week. If I don't do something drastic now, I'll never get him, I might as well give up."

"Vittoria," I said, "you could sleep with Flaminio in Francesco's own bed, and he wouldn't care. He'd thank you for it. You'd be helping him break the Captain down."

"It's the only way," she sighed.

That night, on stage, she invited the Captain to her tent.

The next morning, when she came to see me, I knew at once that her little trick had failed. "I should have listened," she said. "Francesco *didn't* care. Flaminio and I walked right past him last night. I grinned in his face. But this morning, he treated me just as if nothing had happened. He kissed my cheek, and asked me how I'd slept.

"Pantalone," she said, "I've given up hope." Then Vittoria shrugged her shoulders in such a bitter way that I suddenly saw how she would look when she was very old.

"As for that pig Flaminio," she continued, "I didn't even get a good lay out of it. The old fool couldn't do it. Flaminio Scala, the strongest of the strong—his thing flopped around like an overcooked noodle! All night, he tried and tried, rubbing himself against me like a flea-bitten dog. Just before dawn, our brave Captain put his head in his hands and cried."

I knew that Vittoria was telling the truth; and it occurred to me that her story was a weapon which I didn't want Andreini to have. So I tried to make a deal with her, in a way she could understand.

"Vittoria," I began, "do you know what a premonition is?"

"Of course," she replied, always proud when she knew the answer to anything. "It's a warning from the future."

"Well then," I said. "I'll tell you something. I've just had a premonition.

"If anyone else in this troupe hears that about Flaminio, if anyone else learns that he has been cursed in that way, a terrible spell will descend upon all of us. Our souls will fall under the power of the devil, who'll control us like marionettes. Do you want that to happen, Vittoria? Can you understand that you must keep this a secret?"

"Yes," she whispered, her big eyes wide with terror.

But I needn't have worried; over the next months, Vittoria barely talked at all. She gained weight, became dull, slow on her feet. She spent most of her free time sleeping. Often, she'd go on stage without combing her hair. She stopped coming to see me. She was so melancholy, she no longer had the energy to join the others in taunting me.

Gradually, her Inamorata became less and less attractive. By spring, the audiences never applauded her. There was something in the way she looked at the Lover which was too disappointed, too unhappy, too real. It unsettled them, embarrassed them; they felt they were watching a part of her life which they shouldn't have been allowed to see.

The rest of us worked our hardest to make up for Vittoria's failure. But there was nothing we could do. The crowds grew thin, the cashbox empty; once again, we were on the edge of starvation. I was tired, hungry, forced to waste my energy convincing those fools that I couldn't give them credit.

Of course, it was Andreini who finally brought it up, that night he called that awful meeting.

"As much as I love Vittoria," he said, getting straight to the point, "I regret to say that I can't play opposite her any more."

Vittoria was sitting in a corner. I couldn't look at her. I couldn't bear to imagine what pain Andreini was causing her. I wanted to defend her. But I was watching, from the edge of things; it wasn't my place.

"You're right, Andreini!" shouted that bastard Brighella, who was never a great friend of Vittoria's anyway. "We might as well put a lump of dough on stage, for all the popularity she's earning us. And a lump of dough would eat less, that's certain."

Armanda nodded vigorously. I was surprised she didn't chime in, for she'd always hated Vittoria. But the dwarf was in a strange state in those days.

"Vittoria's been with us longer than you have," protested the Captain. He knew that Andreini was right; but he was being torn in so many directions, he didn't know what to do.

"I'm quite aware of that," replied Francesco. "But I'm afraid

I'll have to look for some better setting in which to display my skills.

"Besides," he added, "our sweet Vittoria won't have to suffer. I've used all my influence to find her a job as a barmaid, at a local inn, where the owner's wife is a special friend of mine."

The decision had been made; there was no way Flaminio could object. "My apologies, dear lady," he said to Vittoria. He went over to her, and offered her his arm. As they walked slowly away, leaning on each other, Vittoria seemed too numb to acknowledge me; and I couldn't meet her eyes.

So that was how I lost my only friend, my only connection with the others, my small, inadequate portion of love. These days, I'll admit, Armanda's pleasant enough to me, Columbina's kind. Isabella does her best to make me feel included; but she's fighting against my nature, against impossible odds.

That night, when Flaminio returned after showing Vittoria to her new home, he was a changed man.

"It's the beginning of the end for him," I thought. "This time, there'll be no sudden comebacks, no wondrous repentances, no miraculous reversals.

"Andreini's won at last. He's humbled the Captain, made him dismiss the woman he loves, made him change the casting of the troupe. He's taken everything but the Captain's title.

"He's turned Flaminio into a eunuch," I thought. "What else does that snake Andreini have in store?"

And I soon found out.

"Andreini," said Flaminio, in a strained, tired voice. "We need to find a new Inamorata."

"Just to prove that I have only the best interests of the troupe at heart," replied Francesco, "I will take all responsibility for finding a new actress."

The very next morning, he appeared in our camp with Isabella.

IV • FRANCESCO ANDREINI

LADIES AND GENTLEMEN. When Francesco Andreini was a young man, he spent ten years traveling the world. He was captured by the Turks, sold into slavery at the Pasha's court. He slept in the perfumed palaces of India, scaled the Great Wall of China. It would take another lifetime, ladies and gentlemen, just to tell the story of his adventures. But permit me this one indulgence.

Once, in the course of his travels, Francesco Andreini chanced to meet a wise old Jew. Not a miserly bore, like our Pantalone here, but a true patriarch—an Abraham, a Moses.

In theory, the patriarch was a hermit. In fact, however, his mud hut was always crowded with people, who brought him gold and flowers and traveled eighty miles across the desert to hear him tell the Bible stories which he made up out of whole cloth.

He was a stooped, shriveled old man, with a long, sparse beard. But, the moment Andreini entered his well-kept little room, he began to chatter away in a bright, clear voice.

"Tell me," he asked, "have you ever heard the story of David and Absalom?"

"Of course," replied Andreini. "Priests like nothing better than preaching Bible to boys like me."

"Well, forget what they told you," said the patriarch, scowling and waving his hand irritably. "Because it didn't happen that way. Absalom wasn't angry about a woman, or greedy, or malicious, or power-mad, or any of those other things which the Holy Book implies. Listen:

"Long ago, a few minutes past midnight, David rushed into Absalom's room, and shook his son awake.

" 'Absalom!' he cried. 'I have just had a dream. I dreamed that our kingdom would last forever, that Solomon would build a temple which will stand in Jerusalem until the coming of the Messiah!'

" 'That is wonderful,' murmured Absalom sleepily, trying to clear the fog from his brain.

"After David returned to his room, Absalom found himself unable to sleep. He lay awake, feeling truly happy for his father, hoping that his vision of the future would come true. But at last, Absalom drifted off, and had his own dream.

"He watched the temple of Solomon leveled by foreign armies. He saw the kingdom of David reduced to rubble and dirt.

"The next morning, when Absalom awoke, he knew that he had to change things, to take them into his own hands, because his father's vision was a lie. And that was the day he began his unfortunate rebellion.

" 'Oh Absalom, my son my son, would God I had died for thee.' Ah, what beautiful lines," sighed the patriarch. "If only I had written them myself . . . "

"Why are you telling me this?" interrupted Andreini.

"Because," replied the old man. "You are a boy looking for a father. That is why you are roaming the world, that is why you came all this way across the desert just to see me. And, if you ever find what you are seeking, you will do well to remember the story of David and Absalom."

"A father is the last thing I am looking for," muttered Andreini, and stalked out the door, furious at the patriarch for having wasted his time.

You are a clever audience, ladies and gentlemen. You know the connection, without my having to tell you. Of course, you are saying, Flaminio Scala *was* like a father to him, in those early days.

But if I never thought of the patriarch's story, perhaps it was because Flaminio's dreams seemed to be exactly the same as mine.

Sometimes, in the evenings, when the troupe was camped beside the road, Flaminio would lead me off for a walk in the meadows. Putting one arm around my shoulders, he would talk quietly, with none of that bragging he did in public. He would tell me about his hopes for the company, about the time when we would take our rightful place among the great artists of the world. And, whenever we rode into a new city and passed one of those gigantic equestrian statues they were always erecting in those days, Flaminio would spur his horse up next to mine, and point to the huge bronze soldier.

"Francesco," he would say, "in ten years, they'll tear down that monstrosity, and replace it with a monument to Flaminio Scala and his Glorious Ones."

I believed every word of it, I swallowed it whole. I accepted Flaminio's vision so completely that I was grateful, I was flattered just to play the acrobat, to dance and tumble while the great man acted. And it was within that dream that I flowered, that I developed my art, my talent, all the skills I was later obliged to use against him.

If that dream had come true, perhaps *I* might have been the one Flaminio's ghost would have chosen to visit. Perhaps it would have been me, instead of that silly little Armanda, whom he would have entrusted with the survival of his soul.

But there was no way that things could have remained the same. For, at the time, I considered myself a young man of enormous experience. I was practical, worldly, I knew all the hands life had to deal. I thought ahead, I knew the consequences of things, I saw through dreams like panes of clear crystal.

And so the time had to come when I would see through Flaminio's.

Let me suggest: Francesco Andreini always knew the consequences of choosing a man like Flaminio Scala for a father. Why else would he have bothered to hide his greatest talent? Why else would he have concealed his skill as a trickster and deceiver, if he had not known that he would eventually be forced to use them?

Let me suggest: Francesco Andreini did not *want* to know it, it took him years to admit the truth. But gradually, during that trip to France, during the time of Flaminio's pitiful passion for Vittoria, Andreini came to understand that the Captain was not man enough to lead the troupe. Like Absalom, he began to realize that his father's vision was a lie, and that he had to fight to change it.

The decision was a costly one, bought with sleepless nights, sweaty palms, long, tortured debates. Awake in my bed, I was still Arlechino, shifting my weight back and forth from one foot to the other.

I could hear the sound of my own heart. "He's been kind to you," it said. "He's given you a trade, a home, a life, he's taught you everything he knew."

But my mind was cold, logical, unmoved. "That's all very well," it said. "But strictly beside the point. The important thing is that Flaminio Scala has no practical experience. You know his type: he was a rich boy, a mama's boy, maybe even a college boy. Those people have never been out on the streets, they've never

FRANCINE PROSE

learned anything. You can hear the wind whistling through their empty heads. If Flaminio knew anything about men, he'd never have done so badly when he tried to bargain with those Huguenot kidnappers. If he wasn't so inexperienced with women, he'd never have gotten involved with a woman like Vittoria. There are great things for this troupe to do on earth, Francesco. But nothing will ever be accomplished by a man with his head in the clouds."

"But Flaminio Scala has made The Glorious Ones what they are."

"Small time," replies my mind. "He's made you small time. And it's all the fault of that damned improvisation. The season for that has passed, Andreini, and you know it. It's not good enough any more. It's not reliable enough, there's too much room for error. In order to do the things you want, the plays must be written out in advance, scene by scene, line by line. And Flaminio will never agree to the change. He's dedicated to the improvisation, his whole life's an improvisation, he cannot see the ends of things."

Not even my heart can find an answer to this.

"And another thing." My reason is hammering away at me now, like a lawyer. "Vittoria must go. That dumb slut is the weak point of the whole troupe. She, more than anyone else, was responsible for our expulsion from France. That French Cardinal felt uneasy just being in the same room with those big breasts, that hot body. We need another kind of actress, Andreini—someone more refined, more delicate, someone who will make the churchmen lose their hearts despite themselves. We need someone who will drive the aristocrats so crazy with love that they'll gladly risk excommunication just for the sight of her."

In the end, however, my heart and mind always came to the same conclusion. The fault lay not just with Flaminio, or Vittoria, or the improvisation. Something else was missing—The Glorious Ones needed something else, something elusive, mysterious, passionate, spiritual. Both of them agreed; but, at that time, neither knew what it was.

By the last days of that trip to France, I knew all the lies in Flaminio's dream, all the ways it had to be changed. Several times I tried, and failed. I tried in that freezing cave, again on the journey home. But I couldn't do it. My heart was working against me. And I didn't have the power.

And then, on the night after that absurd performance in the girls' orphanage, Flaminio himself offered me the power like a swig from a jug of wine.

Things were strained between us then, after my two abortive rebellions. But neither of us could admit that all the closeness had ended. And so, though there was little money for wine, Flaminio would occasionally manage to squeeze a few extra cents out of Pantalone, and would invite me to the cafe for a friendly drink.

Perhaps even wily old Pantalone was somewhat befuddled by the strange events of those days; on the night I am remembering, Flaminio's pockets were bulging with silver. I had not been drunk in a long time; it was a good feeling. After we had been in the tavern for almost an hour, I felt free enough to ask Flaminio the question which had been plaguing me all evening.

"We have been friends for many years, Flaminio," I began, in that way you can say such things only when you're very drunk. "Like that," I said, putting my two fingers close together.

"By now, I've learned that an old devil like you often has his own sly secret reasons for doing things, reasons quite different from the ones you tell the troupe. So I am wondering about the real reason you adopted that mangy little orphan, Armanda.

"I can't quite believe that the answer lies in those nasty little jokes you made about her ugliness, Flaminio. Certainly, we've seen thousands of uglier girls in our travels. Nor do I believe what you said to the others, later, about the adoption being your ultimate act of repentance; if you were really serious about the repentance, one visit to the confessional and two thousand Hail Mary's would do just as well. So tell me, Flaminio: what is it? Why did you do it?"

Flaminio draped one arm around my shoulders, just as he used to do in the meadows by the camp. "I will tell you, my son," he said, in that familiar, slurred, drunken way of his. "You know what an upright, honest man I am, what a true Christian, what a brave soldier of morality. You know that I have fought injustice wherever I saw it, fought to expose untruth and hypocrisy whenever I found it.

"Well, that is what moved me, my boy. I took one look at those hypocritical nuns, trying to hide that unfortunate little girl. One look at those brides of Christ, trying to disown His ugly child. And, right then, I resolved to adopt the poor little thing—to make them recognize her, acknowledge her, even if only to deliver her to me." Flaminio paused dramatically, to let his words sink in.

"One thing I know about you, Captain," I said, "is that you are a shameless liar. Go on, have another glass of wine. Maybe it will make you tell the truth."

We drank silently for a few more hours, each involved in his own thoughts. I assumed that I would hear no more on the subject. And then, just as the tavernkeeper was beginning to scratch his head and yawn loudly, Flaminio Scala began to tell a story which at first seemed to have no relation to my question.

"Many years ago," he said, "when I was the most dashing, the most handsome, the most sought-after young man in Europe, I had occasion to travel from Florence to Perugia. As I boarded the coach I noticed that the only other passengers were two nuns, robed completely in white. They were seated next to each other, perpendicular to the window.

"I sat down across from them, and stared at them with the prurient curiosity which healthy, normal men always have about nuns. But their heads were lowered; they were silent, as nuns traveling from place to place usually are. Thus, as the coach got under way, I soon forgot their presence, and began to regard them as dispassionately as I might have regarded two white sacks of flour.

"You can imagine my surprise, then," said Flaminio, "when, for no apparent reason, the nun seated nearest the window began to shriek at the top of her lungs.

" 'Saint Eulalia's bloody breasts!' she screamed. 'Saint Sebastian shot full of arrows! John the Baptist's headless stump! Saint Theresa Whore of Jesus! Mother Mary's womb!'

"Jumping and thrashing about in her seat, she went on in this way for what seemed like an eternity. All the while, her companion murmured soothing syllables, stroked her arm gently, did everything in her power to calm her.

"What a spectacle it was, Francesco," said Flaminio, grinning as he leaned towards me. "What a show! I could hardly keep from howling, I nearly choked.

"The only thing which prevented me from exploding was the fact that the nuns' cowls had fallen back in the course of the commotion. And, for the first time, I could see their faces.

"I saw that the screaming nun was a woman of about forty. Her features were almost handsome, her eyes were black and wild. But the muscles around her mouth had that slack, toneless quality which so often disfigures the faces of madwomen.

"Her companion, however, was a perfect angel of no more than eighteen. And, though the crazy woman initially engaged my curiosity, it was the other to whom my eyes kept returning, again and again.

"Like all young, beautiful nuns, she became somewhat nervous under my scrutiny; but she did not speak until the elder one had fallen silent.

" 'She has been a good nun for many years,' she began, as if apologizing for her sister's behavior. 'For that reason, our abbess does not wish to put her in an asylum. But she is too much for us, in the city, and we are hoping that the mountain air will do her good. That is why I am taking her to Perugia.' "

" 'A sad case,' I nodded sympathetically, and the pretty nun again bowed her head. But I continued to stare at her, thinking how typically inhuman of the church it was to send such a delicate young thing on such a frightful mission.

"Suddenly, the old nun began to scream again.

" 'Stop leering at that girl!' she yelled, glaring at me. Then, as her hard, bright eyes seemed to widen with recognition, she stared into my face and screamed even harder.

" 'As your mother,' she cried, 'I command you to stop leering at that girl!'

"Needless to say, Francesco, I was somewhat embarrassed. 'Whatever you say, Mother Superior,' I whispered, thinking to humor her private delusions of authority and grandeur.

" 'I'm not any Mother Superior!' shrieked the nun. 'I am your real mother, your physical mother, who bore your ungrateful body twenty-five years ago!'

"Of course, I realized that even a crazy woman could easily have guessed my age. Still, I was anxious to hear what she had to say. There is some brave, daring strain in me which has always hungered after thrills of that sort, even if they must come at the expense of an uncomfortable scene.

" 'What do you mean?' I asked her.

" 'Twenty-five years ago,' she began, straight out like that, 'I had a lover who looked exactly like you. Two eggs from the same chicken could not have appeared more similar.'

"She had stopped shrieking, and her voice was quiet and controlled. 'I was still a girl,' she continued, 'younger than this young one beside me. When my parents learned about the love affair there was a scandal, and they arranged to have my lover exiled to a distant province. Nine months later, when I gave birth to you, I was packed off to a convent—a terrible place, where we were forced to sleep in cold, stone coffins, lined with moss. And you were sent to be raised by my married sister and her husband. *Now* do you believe that I am your mother?"

" 'No,' I replied. 'You could have told that story to anyone. There is not a shred of proof anywhere.'

" 'Well tell me, then,' she continued. 'Do you look anything like the man you assume to be your father?'

" 'No,' I admitted. 'But such things are extremely common.'

" 'Tell me this, then,' she went on, her voice growing slightly louder. 'Have you never had the feeling that your mother and father were not your real parents?'

" 'Of course,' I said. 'All children have such fancies at one time or another.'

" 'Then why do you refuse to admit that I am your real mother?!' she demanded.

" 'Because it is not the truth,' I answered, trying to stay calm.

" 'It *is* the truth!!' she screamed. 'I am your mother! Why will you not acknowledge me? Do you want me to tell you how you felt inside my womb? Do you want me to describe the pains, the blood that flowed at your birth, the sac of water bursting inside me? Do you want to know how you nearly ripped me apart, how you strained and tore my body in the labor? What must I do to make you believe me?!'

" 'There is no way,' I said. And, though I was the most courageous young man in all Europe, I trembled a little beneath the force of her rage.

" 'I have an idea!' she cried. 'Let us take off our clothes, right here in the carriage, and compare scars and birthmarks until we find one that matches!'

"At that point, the younger nun became terribly alarmed, and again tried to soothe her companion. But the madwoman would have none of it.

" 'All right then!' she shrieked, in a final burst of fury. 'If you will not accept me, I will curse you! You will come to a frightful end, my son, you will perish in obscurity! You will have a miserable fate, which will haunt you all through eternity! And the instrument of that fate will be a woman from the convent, like myself! My sisters will avenge me, my son, you will live to regret this, you will see!'

"And that was the last thing she said to me," sighed Flaminio Scala, exhaling his sour, alcoholic breath in my face. "She was silent for the rest of the journey. The coach reached Perugia, the nuns and I walked off in opposite directions, and never met again."

After Flaminio had finished his story, I stared into his eyes, for a long time. Then, I spoke.

"Do you think she might really have been your mother?" I asked, very softly.

"I don't know," he replied. "There was no evidence to support her claim. And I would hate to think that I have been cursed so harshly by my own mother."

Flaminio laughed, as if to show me that he took it as a joke. "But the fact is," he continued, growing serious again, "as I looked into the crazy nun's face, I saw that her features looked so much like my mother's that she could very well have been her blood sister."

At that moment, Francesco Andreini understood why the Captain had taken Armanda into the troupe.

In adopting a girl from the convent, he was opening his arms wide to embrace his worst fate. He was challenging his mother's curse.

Of course, he was hedging his bet. Why else would he have chosen such a pathetic little creature, who could do him so little harm? He did not want to take too much of a chance. Still, he was tempting destiny at one of the weakest points of his life. And Francesco Andreini admired him for it.

But Andreini also knew that Flaminio Scala had given him the power to destroy him.

That night, after we returned to the camp, I lay on my mattress, trying to sleep. And the whole scheme came into my head, from beginning to end.

I saw it all. Naturally, there were chances, risks; things might not go as I desired. But I was a man of great practical experience, I knew the consequences. If my plan succeeded, I knew that I would win.

The next day, I began those little tricks with Vittoria; later, at Perugia, I showed my hand. She was so easy to twist and turn, poor Vittoria. I feel sorry now, that I had so much power over her, that I could not understand how she was suffering on my account. But, at that time, everything was in my control. Her experience was one which I had not yet had.

Flaminio, on the other hand, was a difficult one to deceive. It is a tribute to him, how hard I had to *work* in order to trick him. Perhaps I would have failed, had I not had his own dreams and madness working on my side. And certainly, I would never have succeeded, had I not seen the end so clearly.

For already, I had found the woman to take Vittoria's place.

Isabella was hardly a woman then. She was sixteen years old. Francesco Andreini had first seen her leaving her house in Venice; and, because he was still such an adventurous young man, he arrived on her respectable doorstep that evening. He presented her parents with a hand-lettered card, introducing himself as Count Francois of Grenoble, and stating that he had come to court their lovely daughter.

Luckily for Andreini, the girl's family had never met a genuine French count. And the five languages he had learned in his travels permitted him to carry off the charade by muttering to himself in French, while speaking Italian with an accurate and perfectly charming Southern French accent.

Believing him completely, Isabella's parents allowed him to pay formal court to their daughter. He visited her regularly, sat and chatted politely in the main parlor. And, whenever the troupe went on tour, he invented some excuse, some aristocratic business which required him to be absent from Venice.

Andreini was charmed by Isabella. Never had he seen such

an intelligent, beautiful, graceful girl. When he was away from her, she was often on his mind. He would remember some clever thing she had said, and burst out laughing.

But at last, after his suit had dragged on for almost two years, Isabella's parents grew concerned, and felt obliged to press him concerning his intentions. Andreini, who always saw the consequences of things, knew that his casual game could no longer continue. And, in a typical act of high-mindedness and nobility, he decided to explain himself to poor Isabella, and to stop ruining her prospects for a decent marriage.

One night, after her parents had mercifully left them alone for a few brief minutes, Francesco took Isabella's trembling hand in his. "Isabella," he whispered, "I have a confession to make. I know that this will come as a terrible shock to you, but I am not Francois, Count of Grenoble."

"I know who you are," laughed Isabella. "You are Francesco Andreini, the actor. Three weeks before that first evening you came to my house, I saw you perform in the plaza. After that, I took to entering and leaving my home at the times I thought you most likely to pass by. I courted you well, Francesco," she said, smiling sweetly. "Don't you agree?"

I should have known right then. I should have seen that Isabella was more clever than I, that she was a woman to be wary of. But you do not think such things at the start of love. Your vision is clouded; for a moment, you cannot see the consequences.

At that instant, when Isabella revealed the fact that she knew my true identity, the only thing in my mind was that she was the perfect woman for The Glorious Ones.

So I prolonged my visits to her home as long as possible. At the same time, I stepped up my efforts to have Vittoria dismissed from the troupe.

Naturally, I succeeded. Vittoria was fired, and I persuaded Isabella to elope with me, to marry me, to join the company. And, through her, I conquered Flaminio.

I succeeded because I had a careful design. I had it all planned out, through the very last scene, the very last word I spoke in that eloquent introduction of Isabella.

We performed it theatrically, Isabella and I; there was no improvisation in it. Completely shrouded in a hooded black cloak, she followed me into the camp at dawn. I awoke each member of the company, one by one, and led them out into the clearing.

"Ladies and gentlemen of The Glorious Ones," I began, when they had gathered around us. "Beneath this mysterious cape is the most remarkable woman in the world. She is the cleverest since Cleopatra, the most beautiful since Helen, the bravest since the destruction of the Amazon kingdom, the most spiritual since the Blessed Mother herself. She is graceful as the swan, as musical as the nightingale, as sly as the cat, as fierce as the tiger. Whole nations have been sacrificed for women with but a mere fraction of her charm. Empires have fallen for women unfit to wash her linen.

"Perhaps you are wondering where I discovered such a treasure? All I can tell you is that the story of our meeting is far more romantic and dramatic than any play yet written. I cannot even reveal the truth to you, my dearest friends. For there are certain important personages involved, certain indiscretions, certain crimes against public morality which might place us all in mortal danger.

"All I can tell you is this:

"Several months ago, I had occasion to visit the strictest and most prestigious convent in all Venice. It was a fearsome place, as I'm sure you can imagine, where tender young girls were forced to spend the nights of Lent in stone coffins lined with moss.

"During the course of my visit, as I dined with the vicious old abbess, I happened to notice a beautiful young woman scrubbing the floors beneath our table. Deftly and discreetly, I passed her a note, declaring my admiration. And it was then that our courtship began.

"Each day, I stood beneath her window, gazing upwards. She, in turn, stared back at me, with longing, pitiful eyes.

"At last, I could stand it no longer. I rode up to the convent on my stallion, bent the iron bars on her window with my bare hands. I saved her, rescued her, made her my bride.

"Ladies and gentlemen of The Glorious Ones, may I present to you: Isabella Andreini, our new Inamorata!"

For a few moments I paused. I had delivered my greatest lover's soliloquy, which far surpassed any of those I had ever spoken on stage in praise of the Inamorata. I watched the expression which passed across Flaminio Scala's face when he thought about this new woman from the convent. Then I raised my arm high, and swept the cape from Isabella.

Many years later, when Francesco Andreini looked back on that scene, he found himself remembering something which he had long forgotten. He remembered this:

During Andreini's visit to the desert patriarch, so long ago, the old man had told him not one story, but two. The second was a legend about Adam and Eve.

"Eve was not fashioned from Adam's rib," the patriarch had said. "She was created in another place, a distant country. But one day, after Adam had been alone in the Garden for several months, she knocked on the gates of Paradise.

" 'Who are you, and what do you want?' asked Adam. For, though he could not help noticing Eve's beauty, he had experienced nothing, in those first months, which might have prepared him to deal with strangers.

" 'I am Eve,' the woman replied. 'I want to come inside the gates.'

" 'What will you do here?' asked Adam.

" 'I will bring you suffering,' she answered. 'I will listen to the snake, and eat the apple. I will introduce evil into the world.'

"And Adam, who had at first been undecided about this newcomer, immediately opened the gate and admitted her to Paradise."

V · DOTTORE GRAZIANO

AND DID FRANCESCO ANDREINI'S BEAUTEOUS BRIDE throw back her head and begin to warble like a nightingale? Did his pulchritudinous princess shut her emerald orbs and spontaneously compose poetry more elegant than the elegiac odes of Pindar? Did this Helen of Troy, this Cleopatra, this Aphrodite, this Venus—did she transfix us with a look of such heavenly hauteur that we immediately swooned in an apopleptic faint?

No, she did not. I, Dottore Graziano, Professor Emeritus, Doctor of Divine and Earthly Medicine, Healer of the Sick, Scourge of Death, Holder of Degrees from the Universities at Cairo, Paris, Moscow, Athens, Rome, and our very own Bologna, I, Dottore Graziano give you my most learned scientific opinion and my most sacred medical testimony that she most assuredly did not.

On that rosy-fingered dawn, when Francesco Andreini introduced his wife and drew off that burdensome black cloak, Isabella Andreini opened her mouth and began to quack like a duck!

At first, we laughed with delight. Armanda clapped her

hands; Brighella snorted, and expectorated on the ground with satisfaction. How ingenious of Andreini, we thought, to bring such a wondrous comedienne into our troupe.

But, when she refused to stop quacking, when the squawking grew louder and faster and more intense until its cacophony made our aural organs ring, the smiles left our lips.

Francesco Andreini's face turned bright red, as if he were afflicted with some roseate efflorescence, some hideous rash. He shook his wife gently by the shoulders, as if he wanted to slap her, but could not bring himself to do it.

The quacking continued. The thespians stood and gawked. And it is my most careful critical opinion that never, never in our finest moments on stage have any of The Glorious Ones ever delivered such an enthralling and captivating performance.

It was Brighella, of course, who broke our silence. "She's crazy!" he shouted. "She's mad as a hatter! Trust Andreini to bring a crazy lunatic into our troupe!"

"I am sorry, Francesco," said Flaminio Scala. "I am afraid that this unfortunate girl will not do as a replacement for our Vittoria." And, if I may venture a hypothesis based on my preternatural powers of perception, there was a look of relief on the Captain's physiognomy.

But suddenly, instantaneously, Francesco's bewilderment seemed to disappear, and he began to smile. "On the contrary," he said. "It is merely a tribute to her great acting ability that she has managed to fool you all so successfully. Certainly, you should know better, Flaminio my friend—you, with your wide knowledge of thespian technique. You should know that my wife is only pretending to be mad.

"And now, just to prove my point, I will commit her to the observation of our esteemed Doctor Graziano, who, after an interval of several days, will no doubt bear out my contention that Isabella Andreini is saner than any of you."

"Graziano!" cried that cretinous Brighella. "That drunken

fool couldn't tell a genuine madwoman from a rabbit's asshole! He can't even cure the wart on his own forehead!"

The others joined in Brighella's laughter. It was typical of their niggardly natures, for they were always scoffing at my medical knowledge, my latinate language, my boundless store of esoteric wisdom. But, before they could utter another word, Andreini put one arm around his wife, the other about my own shoulders, and steered us off towards my tent.

All the way across the campground, Isabella kept on quacking. I peered at her out of the corner of my eye, calling on my vast experience with madness and derangement to determine the severity of her case.

In my tent, I dissolved my strongest tincture of opium in my finest wine. "For medicinal purposes," I said, taking—I must admit—a small sip from the glass I offered her.

At last, the potion succeeded in sedating her. Then, I rolled back her eyelids, and passed my finger back and forth before her face. I tapped her knee with my gavel, palpated her breasts and abdomen, pushed, prodded, and poked. In short, I examined the patient as I had been taught in the finest universities of Europe.

When at last I had completed my inspection, I turned to Andreini. "She's mad as a hatter," I said, using language that I knew even a layman could understand.

Andreini paced nervously around my tent, looking at my bottles, my packets of dried herbs, my stacks of textbooks and treatises, at all the paraphernalia I had accumulated during my glorious career at the university. He studied the pointed hat, the long cloak, the magic wand I had used when regrettable circumstances reduced me to vending patent medicines in the streets of Florence, where Flaminio found me.

Finally, he spoke. "I had not planned this," he said.

I respected Andreini. He was a practical, scientifically minded man, like myself. And, no matter how it went against my medical ethics, I felt a little—how shall I say—sympathetic towards him.

"Francesco," I said, "if you are hoping to find a way out of this, I would estimate that you have three risings and settings of the sun and moon to come up with one. I can keep her here in my tent, and do my best to ameliorate her lamentable condition. But, after that, I cannot answer for her. For, as you know, things are not quite what they should be these days. The others will not take kindly to the idea of carting a madwoman around with them, like so much extra baggage."

Half-listening, Andreini nodded sadly, and left my tent. I did not see him again for three days. During that time, the actors were quiet, tense, as if they were afflicted with some bilious disorder. They did not have an Inamorata, they could not summon the vital essences necessary to perform.

In point of fact, I wished that they had been a bit more rambunctious then; for perhaps their noisy voices might have drowned out the quacks, squawks, and screams which emanated from my dwelling in intermittent bursts. Because, just as a good physician always accepts and learns from his error, I must admit: those three days marked my first and last medical failure. Despite all my potions, salves, and poultices, I could not cure Isabella Andreini's madness.

When at last Francesco returned to my tent, I placed a comforting hand on his shoulder, and prepared him for the worst. "I am terribly sorry," I said. "But there is nothing that medical science can do to cure her."

"I am quite aware that you will not be able to cure her," said Francesco Andreini, with an odd self-assurance. And it is an incontrovertible tribute to my deep knowledge of human nature that, at that very moment, I realized that Andreini had found a plan.

"But tell me," he continued, before I could reply. "Though I know that her illness is incurable, I am wondering if perhaps medical science has discovered a way to alter the varieties of madness, to control and shape its symptoms into a more manageable form? In other words, Doctor Graziano, do you have the equipment and skill at your command to suppress my wife's unfortunate outbursts, and to turn her into a melancholiac, a depressive, mournful and withdrawn?"

"I have the equipment and skill to do anything! Except cure hopeless madness," I hastily added. "But why would you want me to perform such a peculiar operation? What good do you expect to accomplish? Do you really suppose that the others will love a quiet madwoman so much more than a noisy one?"

"Doctor Graziano," replied Andreini. "If you will swear secrecy according to the most sacred ethics of your profession, I will tell you of an astounding event.

"Last night, as I searched through all my memories, my vast practical experience, and my intimate knowledge of four continents in my efforts to find some solution to this dilemma, the idea of searching through Isabella's belongings occurred to me. Perhaps, I thought, they could furnish some clue, some key to her wretched condition.

"Isabella's things were locked in the chest she had brought with her from the convent. At first, as I pried open the lid, it seemed that nothing in there would prove useful to me; for the box appeared to contain only Isabella's black monastic habit, and a few thin linen shifts. But, when I reached beneath the piles of clothing, I discovered a sheaf of papers, which I eagerly lifted out.

"Imagine my surprise, Graziano, when I examined the manuscript, and discovered the substance of a play! Not some sketchy outline like those our Captain scribbles down, but a complete drama—written out from beginning to end, with all the scenes, stage directions, and dialogue executed to the finest detail.

"I suppose that Isabella must have composed it secretly—by candlelight, I imagine, during those dark nights at the convent. And it would seem that she began it after my secret messages had already filled her head with tales and dreams of The Glorious

Ones. For we are all in there, Doctor; there is a part written in for you, for me, for Armanda, Brighella, Columbina, Pantalone, and the Captain.

"But the most impressive thing of all is the fact that my poor wife seems to have had some awful premonition of the tragic illness which would overtake her. For, instead of a normal Inamorata, there is the character of a beautiful madwoman, a divine melancholiac, so extraordinary and rare that, despite her sadness, despite her enigmatic utterances and long, brooding silences, she manages to win the love and devotion of all the characters, and of all the men in the audience. So what do you say, Doctor? Can you treat my wife in such a way that she can fulfill the requirements of her own role?"

I cleared my throat. I breathed deeply, and puffed out my chest. Let it be recorded in medical history that I, Dottore Graziano, graduate of fifteen major universities, master of the lance and leech, I, Dottore Graziano, felt gratified.

Now, wait. Right now I see a gentleman in the audience turning his back on me, pushing his way out of the crowd, leaving in disgust. I can tell, from his distinguished outfit, that he is one of my esteemed colleagues of the healing profession. And I can almost hear the thoughts in his brilliant brain.

"Why?" he is thinking, "why should this doctor, this physician, this divine practitioner of the healing arts, why should this great man, with such impressive credentials, feel gratified because a stupid actor chooses to confide in him?"

Return to your place, Doctor, and I will explain. I assure you: it was not the confidence which warmed the chambers of my heart. They *all* confided in me, every one of them. They were always bothering me with intimate information about their aches and pains, their worries, their love affairs, their money problems. You know how it is, Doctor: they believe that listening to such things is a part of your job.

No, my Hippocratic brother, the reason for my pleasure was this.

Most of the time, The Glorious Ones pretended to have no trust in me at all. They ridiculed me. They flocked to my tent for medicines and cures; but the moment their symptoms abated, the cruel jokes began again.

"But what about that powder I gave you?" I would argue with Brighella. "Did it not work wonders for your abdominal angina?"

"I threw that powder down the cesspool," Brighella would spit back. "God cured my stomach, as part of His promise to me. And you are nothing but the ignorant quack street-hustler you always were."

And that was how it went on stage. My role required me to strut around in my academic cap and gown, with that monstrous wart pasted to the center of my forehead. I quoted Latin, interpreted dreams, boasted about my research, and offered pompous, philosophical advice on the Lovers' difficulties. The others jeered, pinched my buttocks, battered my cranium with rubber bats, smashed eggs in my face. When I talked of medicine, they doubled over with laughter, grimaced as if in mortal pain, and poked me in the ribs with their fingertips.

Now, my Caducean colleague, can you see why I was so delighted when Francesco Andreini asked me to perform the delicate task of transforming Isabella's madness? It was an admission, a statement, a positive—as we say in the profession—proof. He was banking his entire future on my medical skill, he was gambling with Isabella, with the fate of The Glorious Ones. He could never have done such a thing if he had not had complete faith in me, if he had not known the truth—that I was indeed the greatest scientific practitioner in all Western Europe.

So I acted accordingly, to bear out his trust. I ran to my textbooks, and consulted the ledger in which I had recorded all my research. Moments after Andreini left my tent, I began to dose Isabella with opiates and sedatives. I rubbed the nerves at the back of her neck, attached warming poultices to the small of her back.

By that very evening, she was docile enough to appear with Andreini before the others.

"Fellow actors!" cried Francesco, calling The Glorious Ones together after dinner. "May I present the star of our newest drama, *The Moon Woman*. Now tell me, does not her beautiful face resemble that of the moon?"

No, I thought to myself, it does not. I knew, from my astronomical studies, that the moon had scars, pits, and abscesses in her complexion. As Isabella stood there silently, her eyes downcast, not even a freckle marred her fair cheeks.

For some reason, Andreini had painted her face chalk-white, and rouged the corners of her mouth downward in an expression of tragic sadness. And he had drawn a solitary tear beneath her black-rimmed eyes. It was the physiognomy of a beautiful melancholiac, I decided, but not the face of the moon.

Still, I kept silent, and let Andreini continue.

"I have the script with me here," he went on, "authored by the lady's own hand. Need I point out that its very existence proves her talent, her creativity, her perfect sanity. And the drama itself is so poetic, so compelling, that I will venture to guess that none of you has ever seen anything like it before.

"The plot is an ingenious one. It concerns a madwoman, a ravishing lunatic, whom all the men love, and who is at last restored to sanity by the God of Love himself—"

"Why should people pay to watch such a thing on stage?" interrupted Flaminio Scala, in a bitter voice. "They see enough madness every day of their lives."

The others, who were dissatisfied with Andreini's plan without quite knowing why, immediately jumped at Flaminio's objection, and made it their own. "Exactly!" they cried. "Why should people pay money to hear about something they already know?"

"It is true that they are familiar with madness," argued Francesco calmly. "But we are showing it to them in a beautiful form, which they would love to see madness take. And that is the kind of drama they like best of all."

"But there is no room for improvisation in it," cried the Captain. "It will have no spirit, no life."

"The life is in the lines," answered Francesco. "And, once we have memorized them, we will have the freedom to give the play the spirit it deserves.

"All I am asking," he continued, after a brief pause, "is that we rehearse it for two weeks, learn our lines, and offer a few performances. And then, if the audience does not seem to like it, we can always return to the old improvisations."

The discussion went on for many hours, moving through labyrinths of logic, avenues of argument, dimensions of debate. At last, The Glorious Ones reluctantly agreed. And, the next morning, we began to rehearse *The Moon Woman*.

The plot was simple, the dialogue easy to learn.

Isabella is the beautiful, melancholy daughter of Pantalone the Miser. He keeps her locked in her room, like some wondrous, mad treasure, allowing no one to visit her but Columbina the maid. But one night, as Isabella is staring moodily out her window at the moon, the men of the town catch sight of her, and fall madly in love.

Columbina explains to them that her mistress is in love with the moon. She is always sad, always disappointed, because her passion is hopeless. The moon will not respond, will not come close, will never be possessed.

"Earthly men have no chance with her," says Columbina. "And a bunch of homely fools like yourselves will have less luck than any."

But the suitors cannot be discouraged.

"There are two moons in the sky tonight!" cries Andreini, the Lover, and falls to the floor in a dead faint. Immediately, the Captain begins to bluster her praises in the most grandiloquent language. Knocking loudly on Pantalone's door, I shout out my most complicated theories, prescriptions, and formulas; I promise to cure the Jew's unfortunate daughter. Even Brighella is so deeply moved that he cannot stop cursing and shrieking the vilest insults up at the open window.

Still, Isabella stares at the sky, and will not notice us.

Then, in the final scene, Armanda Ragusa appears, dressed as Cupid, in a striped silk loincloth, a beaded halter, and a feathered cap. Suspended from the scaffolding by wires, the God of Love shoots one of his golden arrows straight at the madwoman's heart. And suddenly, Isabella begins to laugh. She takes a ring from her finger, and throws it down at the ground, at Francesco's feet.

"An old story," Armanda sneered bitterly, the first time we ran through the lines. "The Princess in the Tower. Every schoolgirl knows it."

And she was quite correct. We had all heard the legend before. I knew it as well as the names of the nerves and bones.

But we had never seen it played by Isabella. She learned her part perfectly, my patient. Sitting in the pasteboard window, she bore the same heartrending expression on her face which it bore most of the time. And, in the end, when Armanda appeared, dressed in that outrageous attire, Isabella laughed so naturally that it seemed that she was always seeing that ridiculous sight for the first time.

Andreini was directing her; she did as he said. But they could never have succeeded without my competence, my true art. All through those weeks of rehearsal, I kept her supplied with opiates. Her outbursts ceased completely, and I carefully recorded my observations in the ledger. She took her medicine willingly, almost gratefully. And, when she was not on stage or asleep beneath her husband's blankets, she passed her time in my tent, sitting on a corner of the mattress, staring at the ground.

Often, I would talk with her, though the fact of the matter was that I did most of the talking, and she rarely answered.

One afternoon, however, I decided that it would indeed be a rare plum for the annals of medical science if I could persuade Isabella to tell me the truth about the origins of her illness. And so, broaching the subject as delicately as possible, I at last posed the question which interested me so deeply.

"Isabella," I said, placing one hand gently on her forehead, "tell me, what is the cause of your terrible illness? Did it start in the convent? Did the evil spirits possess you during one of those long nights in the cold stone coffins? Or was it later—did this madness seize you only after your marriage to Andreini?"

"I was married to God before I was married to Andreini," she said, in that strange, cryptic way of hers.

Suddenly, as I looked at her face in the darkened tent, it did indeed seem to be shining with a cold, melancholy light. It was as if the moon had come indoors, in the middle of the afternoon. And it was then that I knew our play of the Moon Woman would be a tremendous success.

Naturally, my thesis proved correct. That first night we performed the drama, I peered into the crowd, and saw that our audience was transfixed. They stared at Isabella as if she had bewitched them, drawn them into her power. Brighella, the Captain, and I received a few grudging giggles; but, by and large, an awed hush hung over the plaza. And at last, when Isabella charmed them with her radiant smile, I saw men, women, and children mopping their eyes with their filthy sleeves.

They continued weeping even during the curtain calls. When Isabella came forward to take her bow, even the most brutish of the inveterate ignoramuses could not help noticing that the sad, distracted expression was still on her face.

They began to murmur with curiosity; as we passed among the crowd, holding out our caps, the people surrounded us, besieging us with questions.

"Is it true?" they demanded. "Is that woman the finest actress in the world, or is she really just as unhappy as she pretends?"

"She is indeed a fine actress," we answered noncommittally.

"Put a few more pennies in our caps, and we will discuss it further."

That night, our hats were heavier with gold than ever before.

Soon, the audiences were demanding six, seven shows a night. We were invited into the homes of noblemen, rich scions of society. We gave command performances at elegant entertainments. Within a few months, we found ourselves being wooed by the titled aristocracy, as they vied among themselves, and frantically outbid each other for the honor of our presence at their courts.

The success made us vertiginous. In three weeks, Columbina grew fatter than a horse. For the first time in our lives, Brighella, the Captain, and I were forced to exercise in order to ameliorate the deleterious effects of excess food and drink. The nobles plied us with money, tasty delicacies, and fine wine. And always, after the performances, they would declare their undying admiration for Isabella, and express their great desire to have her sit at their very own table.

Usually, they addressed their requests to Flaminio, who was still—nominally, at least—the leader of The Glorious Ones.

But Flaminio, who seemed to regard Isabella with some strange mixture of fear and bewilderment, would invariably shrug his shoulders. "I am sorry," he would say. "But you must consult her physician, Dottore Graziano."

You can imagine the pleasure it gave me when the entire room fell silent to hear me venture my learned opinion.

"I too am sorry," I would tell them. "But I am afraid that even the slightest confusion or distraction is contraindicated in our star performer's delicate case."

The nobles took my warning so seriously that they began to walk on tiptoe, as if Isabella were asleep, and they were afraid of waking her.

But they talked about her to their friends. And that is how our second invitation to France came about.

One night, as we were playing for the Borromeo family in their island palace, a man stepped out of the audience. He was a forty-year-old white male. His physiognomy was of the bilious type. He was thin, like a little monkey of the *Rhesus indica* family, and he exhibited a slight asthmatic wheeze as he spoke.

"Mesdames and Messieurs," he addressed us. "Let me introduce myself. I am Count Marcel de Lavigne, of Paris. And I have come to invite you to our beautiful city, on behalf of our beloved king."

Francesco Andreini rushed forward; but, before he could speak, the Captain stepped between them.

"We are flattered by your invitation," he said. "But, quite frankly, the hardships involved in our last journey to your lovely country have made me reluctant to embark on another such venture."

"Hardships?" inquired the Frenchman.

"Hardships!" cried Brighella. "They'd have to drag us back to that stinking country in chains!"

"Be quiet!" Flaminio hissed at him. "Men have been hanged for less, or have you forgotten the sad tale of my three friends?" Then he turned back to the count with a sweet smile.

"Hardships," he repeated. "First, we were kidnapped by those barbarous Huguenots. And then, if that were not enough indignity, our visit was rudely and ignobly terminated by your great monarch himself."

"How long ago was your visit?" asked the count incredulously.

"About five years," replied Flaminio.

"Ah, well then," shrugged the Frenchman, "that explains it. Those were terrible days for my poor country. And it was only an unlucky accident of fate, my dear sir, which brought you to us at such an unfortunate time. Certainly, the forces of chance must have been working against you.

"I swear to you, my good man: Henry is King of France now. We have no more problem with those unruly minorities, and our capital has become a place where great artists like yourself can flourish and grow. I myself will escort you to the city. And, if you do not receive a welcome worthy of the noblest monarch in Europe, you may hold me personally responsible."

So we decided to trust him, all of us, even Brighella. And he kept his word.

He and his private army of soldiers escorted us across the border. The French count was never more than a few steps from my side; he rode beside me, pestering me with inquiries.

"Monsieur," he would say. "Tell me: is that lovely little actress of yours really as sad as she looks? Is there nothing that can be done? Tell me: do you not think that a good man—a wealthy husband, perhaps—might be the answer to all her problems?"

"The Frenchman is in love with Isabella," I decided. As always, I was mystified by the ways of passion—the only thing in the universal system which I did not thoroughly understand. And I decided that he was the one whose madness I should be treating.

At that point, my extraordinary command of logic allowed me to draw the following conclusion: if this is the way a Frenchman responds to Isabella, I reasoned, then our trip will surely be a triumph.

Once again, I was right. The king himself burst into tears at the end of our first performance. "I cannot bear it," he moaned, polluting a goblet of his finest royal vintage with thick, salt tears. "I have never seen such sweetness and such sadness combined in the body of one woman."

Each night, Flaminio's arms were so loaded down with jewels and silver that he could hardly stagger through the halls of the palace. Gold coins dropped from his pockets, rained on the floor in showers.

"Captain!" Brighella shouted one evening. "You have everything you've always wanted—fame, glory, riches. You are at the height of your career, Flaminio. You should be the happiest man on earth!"

"Brighella!" Armanda hissed under her breath. "Stop being so vicious to him!"

For even the most insensitive of us pitied Flaminio, even the blindest could see that there was no pleasure in it for him.

His dream was indeed becoming a reality. But I, Dottore Graziano, the greatest living authority on the interpretation and secret meanings of dreams, I can assure you: it was not coming true in the way he had dreamed it.

Certainly, he was gaining glory, reaping renown. But all the audience's love and admiration was clearly for Isabella, the beautiful melancholiac, the Moon Woman. True, he was famous, but famous only as the leader of The Glorious Ones, the troupe of actors playing supporting roles to Isabella. And Flaminio knew that all the wealth had been earned by Francesco Andreini and his new wife, that they alone were responsible for the differences which had made this trip to France so unlike the last.

Let me sum up my observations: Flaminio had moved to the edge of things, and he knew it. He no longer led the others, no longer played such an important part in our decisions. He was dull, phlegmatic, listless, almost as distant as Isabella. At dinner, he often sat with Pantalone, though neither spoke. And his part in *The Moon Woman* was a small one. He bragged, boasted, swaggered, just as before; but his presence no longer commanded the stage.

All of us saw it, though few cared. Most of them were happy for the wealth, the success; they respected Andreini more than ever, and viewed Isabella with a sort of nervous admiration. They were never envious of her sudden stardom, for they themselves had never been stars.

And I, Dottore Graziano, saw the whole thing as an interesting spectacle, a curiosity, an old drama replayed, The Reduction of the Great to Low Estate.

"That is the way the Wheel of Fortune turns," I would say to myself. "It is just as my professors taught me, in medical school. It is in harmony with the laws of universal concord—a man like Flaminio is ever at the mercy of the turning wheel." And I was careful to record each of the Captain's dispirited words and gestures in my notebook.

Columbina pretended to care for Flaminio. Often, I would see them conversing, see her stroking his head with her fat hand. But it is my well-considered opinion that Armanda was the only one of us who was deeply concerned. Sometimes, I saw tears pop into her eyes as she watched the Captain.

So I was not at all surprised that night, when she came to my room at the palace. Indeed, only a man of my superb sensitivity could have predicted the entire scene so accurately. And, as a testament to my foresight, as a monument to posterity, I have recorded all the details of our little conversation. I have departed from my usual areas of excellence, I have surpassed myself: I have composed a sort of play.

It is long past midnight, but there is no moon in the sky. Isabella sits in my room, on a corner of the silken-canopied bed; she appears even sadder than usual. At last, I gently remind her that it is time to return to Andreini's room. I help her to the door; and, as she glides slowly out of my bedchamber, it does indeed seem that her feet do not quite touch the ground.

In the doorway, she passes Armanda Ragusa, who is coming in. The dwarf raises herself up on tiptoe, peering curiously into Isabella's face, as if to fathom some ineffable mystery. But Isabella, who will not look directly at anything but the moon, refuses to meet her eyes, and continues on her way.

"Armanda," I say graciously, "to what miracle of science or nature do I owe the pleasure of this unexpected visit, at this untimely hour?"

"Stop it, Doctor," replies the dwarf, who could not recognize graciousness if it came up and tripped over her flat feet. "I have come to ask you for a favor."

"Ah, Armanda," I sigh. "You, too, have come to acknowledge the supreme wisdom of my medical knowledge!"

"I have come to kiss your ass if necessary, Doctor," she says. "I will do anything you ask, if you will give me what I want."

"And what is that?" I inquire.

"I want you to do something for Flaminio," she tells me, "I want you to heal his soul, to restore his spirit. I want you to make him the man he used to be, before this Isabella joined our troupe. For I cannot stand to see him this way—a shadow, a ghost. I would do anything to change it."

"Armanda!" I exclaim. "Why such sympathy for a used-up old man like the Captain?"

The dwarf looks at me quickly, nervously, her crossed eyes wandering in their orbits like unsteady planets. "It is not sympathy," she says. "It is just my suspicion of Andreini. I fear the consequences for all of us should he gain complete control of The Glorious Ones. That is why I want Flaminio made strong again."

"I am sorry, my dear," I tell her. "But your beloved Flaminio has been weak—sick, if I may venture a medical opinion—for a long time."

"What do you mean?" asks Armanda.

I can see that I have her interest, that she is waiting for me to expound my thesis, to dredge up the truth from the depths of my extraordinary knowledge.

"I will tell you a story," I say, "a secret, in strictest confidence, of course. For it would certainly be a gross betrayal of my medical ethics to reveal the intimate exchanges which transpire between myself and my patients within the sanctum of my tent."

"Of course," nods Armanda.

"All right, then," I say. "As long as you understand. Well, then, tell me: do you remember that time, not so long ago, when Flaminio was so madly in love with Vittoria—despite the fact, which all of us could see, that her heart belonged wholly to Francesco?"

"I believe that I know which time you mean," snarls the dwarf. "But *I* have always thought that Flaminio secretly despised Vittoria for the slut she was. All that passion of his was merely a charade, for the purposes of the dramas he was playing on stage."

"You may think what you please," I tell her, pursing my lips together. "But I know differently. For, one morning, the Captain—the great Flaminio Scala himself—came to me in tears.

"'Captain,' I asked him. 'What could be wrong? All the troupe knows that you finally got your desire last night—Vittoria went with you to your tent. Surely, you must have passed the night in the most sublime state of delight. So what could be wrong?

"'But wait. Forgive me if I am mistaken, but let me venture a diagnosis. Could it be that you have just discovered the truth, the simple fact which everyone else knows? Could it be that you have just realized that Vittoria only went with you in order to make Andreini jealous?'

"'Dottore,' sighed the Captain. 'Do you take me for a fool? Oh, how I wish it were that simple!'

"'Then what is troubling you?' I persisted.

"'It is this,' Flaminio blurted out. 'I—Flaminio Scala, the greatest lover in the Western World, second in potency only to the great Sheik of Arabia—I, Flaminio Scala, could not perform the act of love with Vittoria Coroniti last night.'

"'I see,' I nodded, avoiding his eyes and whistling softly through my teeth.

"'Doctor!' cried Flaminio, more desperate man I'd ever seen him, even during the course of that first trip to France. 'Help me! Is there nothing you can do?!'

"'I will do what I can,' I said, smiling at the thought that even the Captain himself had at last come begging for a bit of my knowledge.

"And so I began to treat Flaminio's—shall we say—'problem.' I dosed him with tiger's milk, with ground deer horn, powdered shark's fin, dried sea horse, with all the most powerful remedies and aphrodisiacs known to modern medical science. I made a paste of secret, special ingredients, and rubbed it on his temples. I carefully instructed him to avoid exercise and milk products. I advised him to conjure up visions of amorous delights at the moment before sleep, so as to assure the most efficacious dreams. In short, I performed to the utmost limits of my medical capabilities.

"But, each morning, Flaminio came to me with tears in his eyes, and told me that the little fellow between his legs was still as lifeless as the great pharaohs of Egypt . . . "

Suddenly, I notice that I have completely captured Armanda's attention. She is sitting forward on the edge of her chair, straining to catch my every word.

"And so, my dear," I say, very slowly, "you will never guess what I told him."

"What?" asks the dwarf, her voice trembling slightly as she speaks.

"'Flaminio,' I told him, 'it has just occurred to me: the fact that you cannot do it with Vittoria does not mean a thing. When there is such deep passion involved, many men cannot consummate their desire for the mistress of their dreams. They cannot bring themselves to debase the goddess they have worshiped for so long.

"'How careless of me to have overlooked this scientific truth! But now—lest we waste another minute—I will tell you what to do:

"'You must go and practice, Captain. You must find a woman whom you do not love at all, whom you value less than a bit of straw blown by the wind. Surely, there are several such women in the troupe. Armanda will be glad to oblige you, Captain, Columbina as well. And, if they do not agree, there are always the girls who crowd the stage after the performances.

"'You will see, Flaminio. It will be easy for you to do it with such a woman. You will gain confidence and assurance from it, so that the next time Vittoria consents to share your bed, I guarantee that you will not waste another golden opportunity.' "

At this point in the drama, I am surprised to notice tears coursing down Armanda Ragusa's face.

"My dear!" I exclaim. "Why ever are you crying? Can I get you a mild sedative?"

"I'm *not* crying!" snaps the dwarf, a mean look on her face. "It's just that the filthy camphor you always burn is making my eyes smart!"

"Camphor is good for you," I assure her. "It soothes the humors, purges the lungs, strengthens the spirit. But you see, my dear, it is just as I told you—nothing could strengthen Flaminio's spirit.

"You must see, now, how long he has been ill. For years, he has been something less than a man. I fear that he is one of those gentlemen who will always have terrible difficulties with women. And I believe that these difficulties are in great measure responsible for the lethargy which is softening the Captain's bones at this very moment. For, due to some reason which even I do not quite understand, he seems so frightened of our mad Isabella that he can barely bring himself to go on stage with her."

"Then you do not think he is madly in love with her like all the others?" asks the dwarf.

"No," I tell her. "Flaminio feels nothing for Isabella but pure terror."

At this, Armanda seems somewhat relieved. Brushing the tears from her eyes, she rises.

"Thank you, Doctor," she says, her voice still hoarse. "I am grateful for the information. But you and I both know that if you were a real doctor—in fact, if you knew anything at all about medicine—there would be something you could do for our Captain."

Then, without another word, she leaves my room.

As the curtain falls on my little scenario, I am smiling while I prepare for bed.

.   .   .

At this point, I must make a confession. Even I, Dottore Graziano, the most upright and honest practitioner in all Italy, even I am only human. I, too, am quite capable of dissembling, of falsifying, of committing small, trifling, insignificant breaches of professional ethic.

For, that evening, when Armanda Ragusa visited me, I did not tell her the truth.

The facts of the matter were just as I told her. Flaminio Scala had come to me complaining of impotence, and I had advised him to seek out an unattractive woman. But I had misled Armanda concerning my diagnosis of the Captain's *current* disability.

Do you think me an idiot, a mental defective? A man of my deep wisdom could never really have believed that Flaminio Scala had lost all his vitality because of love trouble! Of course not! I knew the truth, I knew that the Captain had finally admitted Andreini's victory, and had given up hope.

But I hated that filthy toad Armanda like the Reaper himself. For she and Brighella had been the worst of them, always ridiculing my knowledge, accusing me of being a posturer, a charlatan, a quack. I couldn't find it in my generous heart to forgive her. And I knew how she worshiped Flaminio, how it would irk her to think that Flaminio had lost his vitality because of Vittoria and Isabella, two other women. So that was the thesis I postulated.

And I suppose that is the way with great geniuses like myself—sometimes, we can predict the future, we can speak the truth without even being aware of it.

For it was not until much later that I realized: Flaminio was indeed terrified of Isabella. In fact, it was not until I, Dottore Graziano, the most rational and logical man on earth, had begun to stand somewhat in awe of her myself.

It happened slowly, I can assure you. Men like myself are

not so easily led astray from the path of reason. Nevertheless, it happened.

Gradually, very gradually, I began to develop a peculiar attachment to my melancholy young patient. Often, I found myself cogitating about her. At night, when she'd depart for Andreini's tent, I found myself wondering what he did in bed with that sad girl.

In the beginning, when she had sat in my tent, I'd hardly paid attention to her; I'd viewed her as another patient, whose case was only slightly more interesting than that of the typical melancholiac. But gradually, I found myself becoming constantly aware of her presence, examining her frequently, wondering what she was thinking about when she stared so longingly at the distant moon.

As you know, I am more than a doctor—I am also an eminent man of advanced and respectable age. Despite the foolish, scorned, cuckolded clown which I occasionally play on stage, Dottore Graziano is in fact not the sort of man who falls in love with eighteen-year-old girls.

Certainly, I might have grown quite confused about my odd fascination with Isabella, had I not been able to diagnose my problem at once: I was not stricken with love, but with an attack of lust. It was the sort of thing which often overtakes men of my years, particularly older doctors with beautiful and helpless young patients.

So I knew what I must do. "Physician," I decided, "heal thyself." And I knew that the only efficacious remedy would be the satiation of my desire.

I did what I knew best. Slowly, subtly, I began to dose Isabella with small amounts of the same aphrodisiacs I had given Flaminio Scala. I fed them to her with her other medicines, so that she would not notice. And I waited patiently for them to take effect.

Six months later, on the trip home from our triumph in

France, I at last decided that my potions must have had sufficient time to do their amorous work. Besides, the company was so joyous then, so wealthy, so certain of success that I suspected that their gaiety might even have affected Isabella.

And so, one night, as we camped just west of the Italian border, I resolved to press my advantage.

Isabella was sitting silently in my tent, staring out the opening in the canvas at the dark sky. In short, everything was just as usual. But, on that night, I began to fancy that she too was stealing sidelong glances in my direction.

So I went and sat very close to her on the narrow bed.

"Isabella," I said, gently taking her hand, "I have something to discuss with you."

She nodded, without moving away; for, as her physician, I often touched her in that affectionate, solicitous way.

On that evening, however, I went beyond the bounds of professional care, and began to run my fingers up the inside of her arm. "Isabella," I said, in my most seductive tone, "has anyone ever told you that you are a beautiful girl?"

As she turned to look at me, there was no expression on her face. Or, more precisely, there was that vague, distant expression, as if she were staring straight through me at the moon.

"My dear," I continued, "from the first moment I saw you, I knew that you were a *real* woman."

Isabella kept on staring, in such a way that, if I had not had utmost confidence in the power of my medications, I might have been discouraged from continuing. But I was unshakeable in my faith.

"The only thing that troubles me, my sweet," I went on, moving my hand up to that soft hollow at the base of her neck, "is the fact that you always seem to be so sad. As your doctor and your friend, I have begun to think that there is only one thing which might really restore you to health and happiness.

"Yes, Isabella, it is just as we play it on stage. It is my final medical judgment that only the power of love can awaken the joyous young girl who lives in secret, deep within your soul. And, as your physician and your admirer, I am prepared, this very evening, to volunteer my own body for the performance of that necessary yet pleasant task."

For a long while, Isabella gazed at me so blankly that I wondered if she had heard, or understood. Then, all of a sudden, she began to laugh.

Even now, the memory of it pains me like an attack of acute gastric distress. But, in the interests of science and history, I feel I must describe Isabella's laughter.

It was rich and full. It filled the tent, and seemed to make the canvas walls bend and sway. It was not a hysterical laugh; I, as a doctor, could most certainly recognize the fact that it was not a hysterical laugh. Still, it did not stop for almost five minutes.

Then, Isabella spoke. Not in the flat, melancholy tone she had used during those long months under my care but, rather, in the bright, confident voice of a healthy young woman.

"Doctor," she said, sputtering and choking with laughter, "I would have to be *crazy* to sleep with you!" And she began to giggle again.

For several moments, I sat there, gasping with amazement, unable to move. Then, I jumped up, grabbed Isabella by the hand, and dragged her out of my tent.

I shouted at the top of my lungs, until all the other actors were awake, and had gathered in the courtyard between the tents.

"Ladies and gentlemen of The Glorious Ones!" I cried. "I, Dottore Graziano, physician and surgeon, graduate of fifteen universities etcetera etcetera, have effected a most miraculous cure. Isabella Andreini is sane again, as sane as the sanest of you. It is all due to my medicine, to my marvelous command of the science of pharmacology and toxology.

"And now, we have no more need of this woman. The play

of the Moon Woman is done, finished, it can no longer be the same. And we need no longer have Isabella in our troupe."

But gradually, I noticed that none of them were looking at me. They were all staring at Isabella, who was smiling sweetly, bowing, greeting each one of them in turn.

"Beloved friends," she said, in a voice so musical and yet so commanding that it brought tears to their eyes. "The play of the Moon Woman is indeed over. We have taken it as far as we can. Tomorrow morning, we will begin rehearsing a new drama, which I have just finished writing."

The thespians were smiling as blissfully as if an angel had come down and kissed them on their foreheads. I stood on the sidelines, clenching and unclenching my fists, unable to forget how she had laughed at me in my tent.

But, after the others had gone back to their beds, Isabella leaned towards me and whispered something in my ear which made all that old desire return. Despite myself, Isabella had reclaimed her place in my heart. I knew I could never be her lover; but, at that moment, I felt myself becoming her servant.

"Dottore," she whispered. "You were absolutely right. It was indeed the power of your love which restored me."

The tone of her voice confused me. Even I, with all my knowledge of medicine, philosophy, and logic, even I, with all my degrees and certificates, even I was thoroughly confused. Because, to this very day, I have never been able to tell whether or not she was serious.

VI · COLUMBINA

"SHE'S NOT CRAZY," I said to myself, the first time I saw Isabella Andreini. "She's driving all the others crazy. *They're* the ones who are crazy!"

God, what a sight: five full-grown men, dancing around her in a frenzy, like chickens with their heads cut off. That's what they looked like to me: decapitated chicken carcasses, twitching in the death throes.

Ugh. I couldn't stand it. So I looked at Isabella instead. And, as I watched her, standing there, squawking like a duck, I saw something in her eyes. It was a certain look, which only another woman could know. And it was not the look of a crazy person.

"Nice work," I thought, "for such a young girl. She's crazy, like a fox is crazy."

A moment later, something else crossed my mind, but I caught myself. "Columbina," I muttered, "you may be clever, but your heart's as stupid as always."

Because my second thought had been for Flaminio.

.   .   .

So I liked Isabella from the very first day. But it was a long time before I got to know her. It wasn't until she'd stopped doing that spooky moon girl routine, until she'd started acting like a normal person. It wasn't until she'd changed her stage part from that of the Moon Woman to that of Isabella, the smart little virgin, out of her mind with love.

Frankly, I envied her those changes. *I* played the same part I'd always played—Columbina, the shrewd servant, the gossip, the expert on sex, the know-it-all. After twenty years of it, I was bored to death, I was ready to quit.

But after awhile, I stopped envying Isabella, and began to feel a little grateful. For she made my Columbina a whole different role.

Playing opposite Vittoria, I'd always sunk straight to my lowest level. On stage with her, I repeated the same stale, stupid jokes I'd traded with the whores at Parma. I became one of those women again, squatting in the street, gossiping, arching huge gobs of spit into the gutter.

Yet with Isabella, it was different. At the age of fifty-five I was light on my feet again, like a dancer. Our scenes together were magical. I waltzed across the stage, counseling Isabella, bantering with her, slandering the ugly old suitors, devising brilliant schemes for her secret meetings with Francesco. The ways I found to insult the Captain, Pantalone, and the Doctor were inspired, positively inspired. I'd never been in better form, not since my salad days in Parma, when I was courted by all those handsome boys who loved me for my wit.

So I thought Isabella and I would be friends, right away. But it wasn't so simple.

Now, knowing Isabella so well, it seems incredible to me, our first real conversation.

It was late, after a performance. Though we'd been playing

together for months, we'd never talked about anything except the scenes, the action, the dialogue. But on that night, when I went to her tent to return a pair of bootlaces, I found her sitting there alone, scribbling in a little book. I knew that the time had come to speak my mind, one woman to another. I knew I should begin treating her like a real person, with a real heart, and a real life, offstage.

"The time has come to ask her," I said to myself. "How did you do it?" I wanted to know. "How did you pretend to be so crazy for so long? How could you fool the man you slept with every night? Where did you learn to act like that?"

But I couldn't bring myself to say it. Maybe you think she had me intimidated, like those quivering men. But listen: there wasn't a man, woman, or child alive who could intimidate Columbina Barzetti, at the age of fifty-five. So maybe it was this:

As I stood there, watching her scribble in that little book, I began to feel that I was in the presence of a lady. I almost curtsied, that's how she made me feel. And it made me polite.

So I wound up playing the same stupid game as the others.

"Tell me, Isabella," were the first words out of my mouth, "what made you get better? I mean, why did you recover from that terrible black mood?"

Isabella stared at me, as if I were talking Chinese. She watched me with those clear, no-nonsense blue eyes. She didn't even blink. Then, she smiled.

"I owe it all to the healing power of Doctor Graziano's love," she said.

My mouth dropped open, I stared back at her, like an idiot. I thought about Graziano—picturing him in my mind—those watery eyes, that alcoholic cherry-nose, that fat paunch, those rotten brown teeth, that bad breath . . . I burst out laughing.

Isabella began to laugh too, holding her stomach and rocking back and forth in her chair. At last, she stopped, and we looked at each other.

She knew that I knew the truth. There was an understanding

between us. I forgot that feeling I'd had before, that I was in the presence of a lady.

And we finally became friends.

But still, it wasn't like it was on stage. Not once did Isabella dance around my tent, shrieking out her love for Francesco, comparing his eyes to the stars, his hair to cornsilk, his muscles to the sinews of an ox. Not that I wanted to watch such a sickening display, in real life. But sometimes, I couldn't help wondering why Isabella never even mentioned Francesco, why she never confided the secrets of her heart.

Yet perhaps, in those days, Isabella simply couldn't get a word in edgewise. For it was I, Columbina the blabbermouth, who did most of the talking. Because there were certain things Isabella wanted to learn from me, things about the troupe, the past, the old days. Isabella was pumping me, and I loved it: Columbina the gossip's fondest dream.

"There's something fishy," I said to myself, when she started coming to my tent, day after day, pestering me for old news. "Obviously, Andreini's told her all this. Why does she need to hear it from me?"

It took me awhile to understand: Andreini was teaching her the history, as if it were the synopsis of a play. But it wasn't enough. What she wanted was the dirt, the dreams, the gossip, the kind of things only women know. And that was why she came to me.

So I told her what she wanted to know. At first, I hesitated, still a little polite, keeping to the ones who no longer acted with The Glorious Ones. Gradually, though, my tongue got looser. I began to talk about Flaminio and his puppy-dog, Armanda. I told her about Flaminio and Vittoria, about Vittoria and Pantalone. It was hard, telling that part, and never mentioning Francesco. But I didn't want to, I was too shrewd. I didn't want to cross that hard-nosed Andreini by challenging his side of the story. So I let her learn about him herself.

It wasn't until much later, of course, that she finally came right out and asked about my own story. By then, my tongue was so loose, I was ready to tell her.

"Bring a bottle of wine to my tent tomorrow night," I said, "and we'll see what I can remember."

The next evening, Isabella came to my tent with a huge flask in each hand.

"Fuel for the memory," I said, pouring a glass for each of us. "Let's see if mine is warmed up yet.

"Isabella," I began, a few moments later, "the sad fact of the matter is that I started out as a prostitute. I had no choice. By the time I was twenty, I had twenty boyfriends behind me. Who would marry me?

"But I was at least a thousand cuts above the other whores in Parma. For, in the fifteen years I walked the streets, I never had to work very hard. I wasn't a common whore, one night at a time. I was too smart for that. I entertained more than anything else—I charmed, joked, and flattered, much like I do on stage.

"And that was why the other whores began to call me Columbina—because I smelled so sweet, like a flower. I wasn't like them, always reeking of dead fish.

"Yet flowers don't last forever, Isabella; that was the trouble with being a courtesan. It's not a lifelong profession, it's not something you get better at, with time.

"One night, I forgot to pull the shades when I went to bed. When I awoke, I saw myself, in the harsh, morning light. I saw the stretch marks on my belly, the thick veins on my breasts, the rolls of fat around my knees.

" 'Get smart, Columbina,' I said to myself. 'Time's running out.' Right then, I knew what I had to do. I decided to find one more wealthy lover. I'd take him for all he was worth, then retire, for good."

"And Flaminio was your last lover," interrupted Isabella. "Bad choice."

"That's the playwright in you talking," I said. "Always knowing the final scene. But you're right. Flaminio Scala was my last lover, and the choice couldn't have been worse. But I didn't know it at the time. His acting was too good.

"It *must* have been good, Isabella. I was a whore, I'd had ten thousand lovers. You'd think I'd have known the ways of the world. And yet I let Flaminio Scala convince me that he was richer than Midas and Croesus put together.

"I sat there like a teen-age fool, listening to him talk about his Arabian emeralds, his Chinese silks, his Indian spices, his Persian rugs. Each morning, when I asked for my money, he'd tell me about the rubies he was going to bring me that night. Somehow, though, he always forgot. Something had come up, he said, his money was tied up. But I shouldn't worry; he'd have it for me, within the week.

"And I kept on believing him, listening to his excuses, letting him come back . . . "

"But why?" Isabella asked. Of course, she couldn't understand. She was thinking of Flaminio as he'd become by then— poor old Flaminio, the cringing hound. She couldn't believe that someone could ever have loved him. "Why?" she repeated. "Why did you let him get away with it?"

It was a long time before I could answer her. "Isabella," I said at last, "they say that women who do it for money have no hearts. They say we have cashboxes in our loins. When we do it with a man, we feel nothing more than if we were dropping a coin into a bank.

"And I suppose it's true. It was that way for me, through most of it. But Flaminio—there was something about Flaminio which made me feel a little more than that. He made me nervous.

"I wish I could say it was Flaminio's big heart, or his generous spirit. But both of us would know I was out of my mind.

"I could never tell the truth to a respectable married woman like you, Isabella, if I didn't feel myself growing a little sentimental, even now. And that tear in my eye seems to make it all right, as if to say, 'Look: I'm a good woman.' For the truth of the matter is this.

"It was something about the way Flaminio touched me, as we lay together on the flea-bitten mattress. There was something that crackled in the air, something that happened inside my own body. It made me nervous, Isabella, it did.

"It seems so long ago, it's hard for me to remember. And sometimes now, as I watch Flaminio slink around the stage like a mangy old dog, it's hard for me to believe that it ever happened at all.

"Even at the time, I couldn't believe it. 'Flaminio,' I used to say, 'what can a rich young man like yourself see in a tired old whore like me?'

" 'I love you for your wit,' " he'd say, with his deep, booming laugh. " 'You're smarter than the princesses of the realm.' "

"And that was how it happened. That was how I became a moon-woman, like the girl in your play. I was just as crazy, just as distracted. I daydreamed constantly, I didn't know if I was coming or going. But, instead of worshiping the moon, I worshiped the man who shared my bed each night."

"I suppose that's healthier," said Isabella.

"Don't kid yourself," I told her. "It's no healthier, just different. Of course, the moon never speaks, never comes close, never responds. But no matter how close he seems to come, a man like Flaminio Scala never tells you the truth. You can't get satisfaction from a man like that.

"But it took me a long, long time to learn it.

"One night, as I lay in bed, drifting off to sleep, Flaminio shook me awake. 'I've got something to tell you,' he said.

"I held my breath. 'There's bad news in his voice,' I thought.

" 'It's time for me to move on,' he said. 'I'm leaving tomorrow, early in the morning.'

" 'Well,' I told him, 'goodbye and good luck. I suppose you want me to forward your bill, so you can pay me later, when you get your hands on all those rubies?'

" 'I want you to come with me,' he said.

" 'As your woman?' I asked him. I was trembling, that's how crazy I was. I could hardly speak. " 'No,' he said. 'That's not in the script. Remember, you're Columbina, the wise woman, the one men admire and fear for her wit. But you're not the one they love, Columbina, not the one they marry. That's someone else's part.'

" 'Script?' I shouted. 'Part? What are you talking about, Flaminio? Have you lost your mind?'

"Right then, he told me about The Glorious Ones—though, at the time, it was just Flaminio and a few worthless friends. Right then, I knew: all that good love-making had just been his way of recruiting me into his miserable troupe.

" 'Go to hell!' I screamed at him. 'You can be the star performer, at Satan's ball!'

"But that night, I discovered something which I already knew: I just couldn't sleep in a bed I'd once shared with a lover. All night long, I tossed and moaned. I talked to myself out loud, to drive Flaminio's ugly face from my brain. And, in the morning, I got up and joined The Glorious Ones."

"And Flaminio?" asked Isabella. "How did he treat you? How do you feel about him now?"

I was drunk, but not too drunk to sidestep her first question. "I feel the way we all do," I said. "I'm sorry for him."

No sooner were the words out of my mouth than I realized my mistake. I *was* too drunk, my tongue had gotten so loose that it had slipped.

Because it was her fault that we all pitied Flaminio, hers and Andreini's. They were the ones who'd changed him, broken his will. Day after day, I watched the Captain shrink, until he was no more than a shadow. And it was all the Andreinis' fault.

So it must have sounded like I was accusing her. "Don't misunderstand me," I said, in the uncomfortable silence which fell between us. "That's the way these things go.

"And you?" I said at last, trying to change the subject. "How did *you* happen to join The Glorious Ones?"

"It was just as Francesco said," she declared, staring straight at me, hard as a diamond. "He rescued me from a convent."

"Isabella," I said, too foggy to pursue it, "why are you always so clear-headed? Why do you never drink as much as me?"

"Because I haven't lived as long," she replied. Then, she got up and walked out of the tent, leaving the half finished bottle behind her.

So that was our friendship. We were friends up to a point, but no further. And that point was Andreini. Her first loyalty was always to him; he'd tricked her well, just like the others. She loved him so much that, between the two of us, the truth had no meaning.

But the fact is: I wasn't so honest with her myself. It wasn't that I lied, when I said that I felt sorry for Flaminio. It was just that there was more to it than pity.

My ties to him went deeper. Of course, I didn't love him any more, I wasn't even sure I liked him. But somehow, I always felt my life was bound to his, in some way I didn't understand, and didn't really like. Maybe it *was* because I'd been in love with him; maybe it was because he was the only one of them who'd known me when I was young. Or maybe it was this:

Aside from Pantalone, Flaminio and I were the oldest ones in the troupe. And, in those last years, when success swooped down on us like a whirlwind, we were the only ones for whom it came too late.

Despite his seventy years, Pantalone loved it; his pouch had never been so full of gold. Brighella was ecstatic, the Doctor was more full of wind than ever. Even Armanda was happy, for suddenly, hundreds of cute young men came out of the woodwork, dying to make love to a famous freak of nature.

But I had nothing to spend the money on; I couldn't buy myself a lover, a child, or a new body. And Flaminio had been cheated even worse. The Glorious Ones had been taken from him; even with all that money, he was poor.

And so Flaminio and I moved over to take Pantalone's place at the sidelines. Like two homely girls at a dance, we stood and watched, ignoring each other's presence. We watched thousands of noblemen drool over Isabella's hand. We watched three trips, to Spain, to France, to England. We watched the testimonials, the tributes, the parades in our honor.

But we were only watching. It was as if all The Glorious Ones were on stage, and Flaminio and I were alone in the audience.

So what I felt for him went deeper than pity. There was some leftover love in it, of course. And there was also some hate, for all those times he'd joked with me like some clever man, and refused to admit I was a woman.

Yet, in the end, it was obvious that no one would talk to him but me. Even Armanda was too busy with her new boyfriends; she'd forgotten him. So I let him come close, in a way I never would, if I'd still been in my prime.

It was hard, being friends with both of them at once. Sometimes, he'd arrive at my tent just as Isabella was leaving. And, though she never insulted him outright, like Andreini did, she always gave him such a mean look that he'd wind up shaking, trembling, stammering for five minutes before he could talk.

"Columbina," he'd whisper. His booming voice had become a bird-croak, he never laughed any more. It was a pity to hear him. "Columbina, they are destroying me. They are taking away my power, the loyalty of the others, everything I have. They are ruining all my dreams of fame and immortality. Because of them, I'll die obscure, unknown. All my work will have been in vain.

"How could he do this to me—Francesco, whom I loved like a son? After all I did for him, how could he turn on me like this, and stick his sword between my ribs?"

"Now you sound like Pantalone," I said, "complaining about his daughter's treachery."

"And her!" cried Flaminio, too upset to see that I was teasing him. "What have I ever done to Isabella? We've hardly spoken. What have I done, that she should treat me this way?

"She's a curse on me, I know it. She is a curse from the past, a curse sent down to punish me!"

"You deserved to be cursed," I told him, "for all the women you've mistreated in your life." I was hoping to flatter him, by reminding him of his amorous career. But Flaminio was beyond flattery in those days. He responded to my little joke with a pained look, as if I'd stuck him with a pin.

"Columbina," he'd whimper, "what shall I do? What shall I do to save myself?"

At last, one night, I lost my patience. I was sick of him treating me like he always did, asking for my wise advice, never loving me, never giving me anything in return. So I spoke my mind:

"Flaminio," I said, "you're wallowing in self-pity, just as you've always wallowed in everything. Listen: you should see yourself acting lately. You creep around the edge of the stage as if you were terrified of the audience's noticing you. It's disgusting to watch.

"Maybe the Andreinis have stolen your power. But they haven't stolen your skill. You can still act as well as either of them, Flaminio. If you don't do it, it's your own fault.

"If you want to keep your fame, here's how to do it: act circles around them. If Francesco is being outrageous, be twice as outrageous. If Isabella is intense, be three times as intense. That's how you'll get your fame back, Captain—as an actor, not just as the manager of The Glorious Ones."

Now, as I look back on that advice I gave Flaminio, my heart hurts. I cringe. I think I should have kept my mouth shut. For, if Flaminio took my advice, does that mean I was responsible for what happened next?

Naturally, I'd prefer to think not. I'd prefer to think that, in those last years of his life, Flaminio was in no shape to take anyone's advice. I'd prefer to think that he was going crazy, and that his craziness was the cause of that last tragedy.

He must have been crazy. Why else would he have done it at a time when it couldn't possibly have made him famous—off season, when there was no one in the audience but street trash?

It was early in the fall. All over the continent the aristocrats were busy moving from their summer palaces to their winter palaces, doing whatever it is that keeps aristocrats busy. They were too busy to give parties, watch plays, or sponsor performances of The Glorious Ones. So we went back to the plazas, where, to tell the truth, I'd always liked it better anyway.

We'd been in Turin for almost a week when I began to notice a peculiar thing about Flaminio Scala.

His acting was improving. His voice had gotten resonant again. His jokes were funnier, his boasts grander, more convincing. He strode across the stage, slashing the air with his sword. When he bragged about the battles he'd fought, the ten thousand pygmies he'd strangled with his bare hands, even I almost believed him.

Everyone in the troupe noticed it; it was just like the old days. Andreini's mouth dropped open. Isabella kept asking me what had gotten into the Captain, for she'd never seen him act like that. And, when she spoke to Flaminio, her face no longer wore that nasty look.

But they no longer met at the entrance to my tent. Flaminio had stopped visiting me, he'd stopped confiding in me. Once again, he began to treat me as he had before—one old man to another.

It hurt me. I felt cheated, abused. And perhaps that was why, on the night of that frightful show at Turin, I found myself watching the tragedy as if it were just another scenario which the Captain had outlined in advance.

It is a hot September night. Isabella, Columbina and the Captain are together on stage. While the Captain valiantly presses his suit, Isabella giggles coyly, cattily. Columbina scampers around, creeping up behind Flaminio's back, mocking him, putting horns on his head.

"My darling Isabella!" cries the Captain. "Why will you not love me—I, who have leveled half the cities of Asia in your honor? Why will you not take me as your true love? Why will you not acknowledge that I, like some noble worm, have burrowed my way into the deepest places of your heart?"

"Because you are so old, Captain," giggles Isabella. "And so silly. Now leave my house. I don't want to see you any more."

"But tell me, Captain," she whispers seductively, a moment later. "What are you doing, later tonight?"

"Nothing, my dear," replies Flaminio, rising to his tiptoes in expectation.

"Well, then," says Isabella, dissolving into gales of laughter, "why don't you take a bath?"

The audience roars. The Captain places one hand across his forehead, as if in mortal agony. Several minutes pass before the laughter dies down. Then, he speaks again.

"Isabella," he begins, with a vibrant quaver in his voice, "if you do not agree to take me as your husband, I shall surely perish, by my own hand!"

"If you're going to kill yourself, Captain," says Columbina, "please, do it outside, so you won't get blood on my nice clean floors."

Without another word, the Captain rushes out the pasteboard door. The two women go to the window to watch him. He stands up straight, spreads his feet wide apart, draws his sabre with a sweeping gesture. He looks up at the sky, and crosses himself. Then, crying Isabella's name, he pretends to plunge the sword deep into his heart.

It was then that the play became real. I ran across the stage, knelt down, cradled the Captain's head in my arms. I heard his quick, shallow breathing. I dipped my finger into the red liquid staining his tunic.

It was not the strained tomatoes we used in duel scenes. It was real blood, flowing in big clots from the Captain's chest.

"Flaminio!" I cried. "Has Andreini tricked you again? We never use real swords, the points are always dull. Did he switch them on you, behind your back?"

"No," gasped Flaminio. "This time, I have tricked him. For now, despite everything he has done to subvert me, I will still become famous. I will be known forever, until the end of time, as the actor who killed himself on stage, who actually did it, whose performance was more real than that of any other man in the history of the theater. People will talk of it, I will be known for it. My body will die tonight, but my name will live forever in the memories of our illustrious audience!"

Obviously, he was crazy. There were only fifty people in the crowd that night—dumb, common yokels. They pressed up near the stage, bug-eyed, chewing their gums as they watched Flaminio die.

Suddenly, the Captain noticed that Isabella was standing above him.

"Whore!" he cried up at her. "I have beaten you! I have beaten the old curse! Now, you will not be able to erase my name from the earth. I will not be betrayed by a woman from the convent!"

Isabella's eyes were flashing. "There is time enough in the world for you to be forgotten," she replied. "There is still time," she said, turning her back on the dying man.

For awhile, it seemed as if Flaminio were right. On the morning after his death, the story was all over the city. Painters sold watercolor medallions of him in the marketplace. He was looked on as a martyr, a saint of art. People came in droves to see the company whose leader had killed himself on stage.

And, despite Francesco's efforts to dismiss the whole thing as a freak accident, even the nobles soon heard of it. And, when the season began again, our rich audiences were more impressed than ever. Those swine were quite charmed by the paradox—a

FRANCINE PROSE

company of clowns whose leader had taken himself so terribly seriously.

But people's memories are short. Within months, Flaminio's last performance was forgotten. We found ourselves playing to crowds who'd never seen him.

I alone have never forgotten the Captain's last scene. And sometimes, it's very much on my mind.

I've been thinking of it often lately. For one thing, it makes me certain that Armanda's story is a lie. How could Flaminio have appeared to her from heaven, in a dream? The old man killed himself, he could never have gotten into heaven. And besides, *I* was the one who cradled his head in my arms during the tragedy. That silly little dwarf was off in another corner of the stage, flirting with some boy from the audience. Why would the Captain have come to her?

And lately, too, I've been thinking about Isabella's part in that scene. Why was she so vicious to him, at the very moment of his death? What had he done to her? Nothing!

I've always thought that the answer lay in her great love for Francesco. She was so loyal to him, so worshipful. She would have killed for him—it was easy, to mistreat a poor old man.

And, for a long time after Flaminio's death, it all seemed to make perfect sense. Francesco was our leader, but Isabella had the power. She was our queen, we loved her. Our feelings for her were out of control. We were more loyal to her than we'd ever been to Flaminio. There wasn't that anger; *she* wasn't the one who'd cast us in those terrible roles. Isabella worked us like puppets, but we didn't mind; we were pleased to be in her puppet show.

But lately, everything's changed. Lately, it's hard for me to imagine that Isabella Andreini is the same woman who said those cruel things to Flaminio.

For Isabella's grown quiet again, withdrawn, like she was in the beginning. She's no longer my friend.

This time, though, I saw it coming.

108

"Isabella," I'd say to her, before she stopped talking to me, "what's gotten into you? Are you having trouble with Andreini? You can tell me. Or is it something else? Am I imagining it—or do I see a funny look in your eye every time that Pietro comes around? You can tell Columbina, she's an expert on these things."

"No," she'd sigh. "It's none of that. It's the moon. I'm afraid that I want the moon."

VII • ISABELLA

SLEEP WELL, PIETRO. Pull the blanket over your head. I want to stay with you all night, but you know how a dream is. One hunger pang, one cat screeching in the yard, and it's gone. You close your eyes, you curl up in a comfortable position, and concentrate on your dream. But it won't come back. My image will dissolve, and you won't be able to hear me.

Here in heaven, we don't have dreams. There's no need for them. But there's no time to talk about heaven now. There are other things I have to tell you, and there isn't enough time.

But maybe there will be time. Maybe you'll sleep all night. After all, you must be tired. I saw you today, marching through Lyons with that huge procession. You were on your feet for hours. The sun was very hot, and the sweat streamed down the back of your neck. I blew on those streams, to cool you. Did you think it was a breeze, Pietro?

I don't think you even noticed. You were too busy looking at the magnificent coffin they'd given me—white alabaster, with silver handles. You could just glimpse my body through the translucent walls. It was as if I'd been frozen in ice, as if I'd fallen asleep inside the moon.

How I wished you could have been one of my pallbearers, Pietro. I hated the way Andreini did it. He wanted it to be another show—an actor's funeral, a real curiosity, like a gypsy's funeral, or one of those Hindu rites he'd seen in his travels. He thought of us as freaks, members of another race; we even buried the dead our own way.

So he decided that The Glorious Ones alone should bear the casket. The Doctor and Pantalone lifted it up on their shoulders; the old men staggered beneath the impossible burden. Francesco bore the whole weight of the front; Columbina took up the back. Even Brighella and Armanda ran along beneath the coffin, jumping up and reaching towards the alabaster in some grotesque attempt to help. It was as if I'd turned into a carriage, a moon-carriage, drawn by a team of outrageously costumed horses.

Yet death has turned me into a simple woman. I didn't want to say goodbye to the world with a circus. I wanted the same thing everyone else wants: eight sad, ceremonious pallbearers, dressed in black. Uncles, cousins, brothers, friends, sons. And I wanted you to be among them, Pietro, so that I could rest on those broad shoulders I used to stare at while you were changing costumes in the wings.

But you alone were left out. There was no reason for it, it was senseless, you were the strongest one of all. Except, of course, that Francesco must have known.

Did you wonder about that today? Did you watch Francesco carrying the coffin, and try to read the truth in his eyes? I doubt it, Pietro. You were never interested in the inside of Francesco's brain, or anyone else's. You were different from the others, in that way; that was why I liked you, from the start.

Besides, you were too distracted by the spectacle around you to worry much about Francesco. For my husband had finally outdone himself—it was greater than his greatest performance, grander than his most lavish production. A state funeral for Isabella Andreini—financed by the King of France himself!

Ten thousand people paraded solemnly through the streets of Lyons, sweeping down the main avenues, choking the narrow back alleys. Five hundred monks chanted the *Dies Irae;* five hundred nuns sang the Tenebris. There were two court orchestras, four military bands. A million lilies, planted in the windowboxes, filled the air with perfume. Banners with my face painted on them fluttered in the wind. Noblemen rode black stallions, soldiers wore black plumes in their caps. Grown men buried their heads in their hands and cried; women keened and wailed. And their children, too young to understand what was happening, jigged to the music of the fife and drum.

It must have confused you, Pietro, I know. It confused me too, for the same reason.

Just three months ago, I thought, I was a woman of thirty, an ordinary woman, sitting in your tent, complaining, bored, dissatisfied. And suddenly, I was dead, and the King of France was hailing me as a goddess!

He spoke well, King Henry. I was pleased, and a little surprised—because, after all, he was a politician, and not a poet. But I suppose some politicians can speak a certain kind of poetry. They can deliver a eulogy which will warm everyone's heart.

And that was what he did.

"The first time I saw Isabella Andreini," began the king, "I told myself that she could not possibly be a mortal woman. I thought that she was surely one of the gods, come down to earth in the guise of a young lady—to steal our souls, through our eyes, and ears."

The king went on to praise my skill as an actress and a playwright. He compared my voice to that of the nightingale, and related a few anecdotes to illustrate the sharpness of my wit. He talked of the success I'd gained, of the honors I'd won. He held up the bronze portraits of me, the commemorative medals. He displayed my honorary degree from the University of Padua, and told how the French Cardinal himself had placed my effigy between a bust of Petrarch, and one of Tasso.

"The only consolation for having the lovely Isabella die so suddenly and tragically in our country," concluded the king, "is the satisfaction of knowing that her remains will sweeten French soil until the Last Judgment."

Though it confused me, I thought it was a good speech. I felt the king meant what he said; I didn't worry if perhaps some of his praise was undeserved. Besides, the sight of a monarch commending an artist is a spectacle which people have learned to associate with noble feelings. The crowd was pleased and proud.

Only my spirit was discontent.

Perhaps I would have liked it better had I not been distracted by the sight of The Glorious Ones, weeping. For I knew that they were only pretending to weep, just as they'd always pretended to love me.

But wait. That's too bitter. Maybe they *did* love me, just as they'd always claimed. Maybe Brighella loved me, and Pantalone, Columbina, the Doctor, Armanda, Francesco. Of course, Francesco. Maybe they could have loved me and still have wanted me to die.

Because that was the truth: they wanted me to die.

Even here, in heaven, where Jesus Himself preaches the Gospel to anyone who'll listen, I find it hard to forgive them. Sometimes, I think it's my punishment. I'm angry at the same sort of thing which so enraged Flaminio—I've been fooled, deceived, I had no idea. I never suspected until the end, when I was so sick, and they came to visit me, one by one.

By then, my fever was very high. It was a turning point; either I would live, and have the baby, or die, taking it with me. The fever made it hard to see them; I was watching them through a haze. I watched Columbina bathing my forehead, the Doctor taking my pulse, Pantalone sighing, Armanda and Brighella

LLLLL

trying to make me laugh. Francesco reassured me, telling me he *knew* I would get better.

But, watching through that mist, I saw something deep in them, beneath their words and gestures.

They wanted me to die. They were directing me to die, begging me. They wanted it so badly that they killed me—not spiritually, Pietro, but physically—physically killed me!

Now wait. You're getting excited, restless, tossing in your sleep. And I don't want to wake you. Besides, there's no time for accusations; they're not important enough.

So all I will say is this: I knew that The Glorious Ones wanted me to die. But I would never have understood why if it hadn't come to me in that fever dream.

Here is my dream, Pietro, my dream within a dream.

I was on stage, about to perform a new play. "How useful," said my dreaming self, because sometimes whole plays came to me in dreams.

But soon, I knew that it was not going to be useful at all. For it was the kind of dream in which I'd never rehearsed, I didn't know the lines, I'd never heard of the play. You know the dream I mean, Pietro; everyone has them.

As always, I felt my heart speed up; an alarm sounded in my head, like the noise I used to hear as a little girl, waking from a deep sleep to see ghosts in my father's house. But, by the end of my life, I'd had that dream so many times that I'd learn to calm myself, to step back, like a member of the audience, to see what sort of play it would turn out to be.

In my fever dream, the drama was a strange one. I played a woman in labor.

All the time, I was aware of the fact that I didn't know what I was doing. Yet the acting seemed effortless; my body contracted rhythmically. There was no blood, of course; it was only a pantomime. And I thought I was doing well, pretending to give birth.

But suddenly the audience began to hiss. They booed, shouted, then left the theater in disgust.

Immediately, the actors gathered around Francesco, to discuss the failure. "Childbirth is too serious," he told them. "It's not the sort of thing from which good comedy can be made."

"That's right," they agreed, turning to me. "You'll have to go, and take the baby with you."

"But I want the child," I said, confusing the play, the dream, real life.

"Then you have several choices," The Glorious Ones told me. "You can be the Inamorata—unmarried, pregnant, desperate to conceal her disreputable condition. You can have the baby painlessly and magically aborted by the Doctor. Or, you can bear it and give it away; perhaps it will come back to you, a stranger, twenty years hence. And there is another possibility: you yourself can be the child, Pantalone's rebellious daughter.

"But you cannot bear the child and keep it, Isabella. You can't be a mother, a woman, for that's not the stuff of comedy.

"So you must go away now, and take the baby with you."

When I awoke from the fever dream, I understood why The Glorious Ones wanted me to die. They were sterile, all of them. It was as if they'd been bewitched, cursed; they made love, but nothing ever came of it. There was no room for a baby in their comedy.

"But what about Francesco?" you're wondering. "Surely *he* wanted the child? It was his baby, his immortality!"

That's the way you think, Pietro, I know. But you're not Andreini. I knew what was in his mind, because I remembered a story he told me, long ago, a story he'd heard in India. It was about Shiva, the dark god, the destroyer and creator, the lord of sex and death.

After ten thousand years of marriage, Shiva's consort, Parvati, the goddess of fertility, decided that she wanted a child. But

Shiva refused to give her one. He loved his wife so much that he knew he would be jealous of the love she gave their own baby. Besides, as he saw it, there were already enough gods and goddesses; the people's libations were hardly enough to go around.

But Parvati was determined. So she fashioned a fat little baby out of chick-pea flour. And one night, as her husband slept, she placed the figure close to his mouth, so that the god would breathe on it, and bring it to life.

Shiva was awakened by the baby's cries. Immediately, he understood what had happened, and became so furious that he raised his razor-sharp sword, and lopped off the baby's head.

Parvati began to weep. "I'm leaving you," she said. "I'll throw myself in the ocean, and swim around with the fish. Or I'll jump into the fire, and dance with the flames. I don't care what I have to do, but I'm leaving."

Shiva knew his wife well enough to realize she meant what she said. "What can I do?" he asked her. "What can I do to make you stay?"

"I want a new head for my baby," she mumbled through her tears.

Seeing that he had no choice, Shiva agreed. "All right," he said. "I will borrow a head from the first living creature I meet."

At that moment, a huge elephant stuck its long trunk into the god's window, trying to steal some of the almonds stored in a silver bowl on the sill.

And that was the birth of Ganesha, the fat, elephant-headed god, who rides a rat, loves fruit, and helps people overcome the small obstacles of daily life.

I can't remember when, or why, Francesco told me that story. Maybe it was in the beginning, when he was coming to my home, courting me with stories, telling me every one he knew. Or maybe it was later, maybe he was talking about something else. Maybe the story was meant as another comment on his great love affair with Flaminio.

But still, I remembered it. And I told it back to him, when I was pregnant, in the midst of an argument.

I was surprised at how angry it made him. For he was being very careful with me then. He was afraid that the pregnancy had unbalanced me, afraid that something terrible would happen, like when I first joined the troupe. So I thought I could get away with anything. But I was wrong.

"I *do* want it!" he screamed at me. "You're the one who isn't sure!"

It would never have made him so angry if it weren't true. But only now, looking down from heaven, do I understand.

Francesco wanted the child, but he wanted the spectacle more. If he'd been given the choice, he'd surely have chosen the state funeral, financed by the King of France. A baby wasn't his idea of immortality, it wasn't part of his plan. But the funeral oration was.

How proud Francesco looked, stepping up on the black-draped podium, after the king had finished speaking. He stood very straight, and threw back his head. There were a few wrinkles in Francesco's cheeks; that mass of bright yellow ringlets had begun to gray and fade. But he was just as tall, his limbs were just as long and sinewy, his hands were as large and graceful as ever. If anything, there was more magic in his body than on the first day I met him. If I hadn't known him so well, my heart would have leapt at the sight of such a handsome man.

"Ladies and gentlemen," he said, in that perfect French which had always made him so proud. "You have heard your gracious king speak of my late wife's genius, her incredible talent. But I alone can tell you about a side of her which no one else knew. I alone can tell you what it was like to be married to Isabella Andreini.

"It was a blessing from God, ladies and gentlemen. She was not only my wife, but also my friend and companion. She cared for me, nurtured me, inspired me. Never was there a more perfect mate. Sarah could not have been kinder to her Abraham, Penelope was no more loyal to her Ulysses. Never once did I need her help, and find it lacking; never once did I call out to her, and find her gone.

"And she was a model of virtue and piety, ladies and gentlemen. For, despite the ugly gossip which often surrounds the female members of our profession, I can assure you: a sister of the convent could not have been more faithful to her lord than Isabella was to me."

Francesco was performing better than ever before. It was the crowning moment of his career. His voice soared, his body trembled with emotion. He could speak proudly, eloquently, because he knew that his words had the unmistakable ring of truth.

And my spirit, hovering over the dusty plaza, shriveled and darkened with misery.

"Francesco," I thought, "why are you saying the very things which hurt me most?

"Francesco," I thought, "did you ever love me? I never knew, I never came close enough. You should never have tried to play the Lover, Francesco. Because you were always Arlechino—the big, half-wild cat, the mystery. That was your proper role. You were split in half, black and white, like the patches on your costume. You were always having those conversations with yourself, between those two sides of you. But I could never come close."

So, even after death, I didn't know the whole truth: was it all part of Francesco's plan? Could he really see the end so well? Did he know that I would lose the child and die, so that he and The Glorious Ones could perform at a magnificent state funeral, financed by the King of France?

Yet perhaps I am making a mistake, crediting him with so much power, believing that he had that terrifying foresight which he always insisted was his. He was a man, after all, not a god. He couldn't see the future.

But we can have as much power as we allow ourselves to

take—Francesco himself taught me that. And that is why I think he knew.

He knew that I would die. He knew he would be able to orate at my funeral. He knew that I'd remain faithful, so that he could honestly praise my flawless virtue. He knew that nothing would happen, on that day I went to visit Pietro Visconti in his tent.

Remember, Pietro? It was three months ago. We were camped in the south of France, on our way to Lyons. I waited until early afternoon, because I knew how much you loved to sleep, and I didn't want to wake you. Then, I walked straight into your tent, without announcing myself.

You were lying on top of the bed. You were dressed, but your boots were off. I was afraid to sit next to you, on the bed. So I sat down on a pile of rags and old clothes, in a corner of the tent. I looked at you, but I didn't speak.

"Is something wrong?" you asked me. (Did you suspect? You must have known, unless it was just my imagination.)

"No," I said.

"What's wrong?" you asked.

"Nothing." I shook my head.

"Oh," you smiled. "It's the pregnancy. You're not feeling well, are you, Isabella?"

"No," I replied. "It has nothing to do with the pregnancy."

But perhaps it did, more than I thought. For I could feel a cold chill, coming up from the earth, permeating the rags and old clothes, creeping up my back. And it bothered me, though such things had never disturbed me before.

So I got up, and began to pace back and forth. But the ceiling was too low. I couldn't stand up straight, and I didn't want you to see me like that, my head and neck bent like a buzzard's. By the time I sat down again, I had no choice but to speak.

"There *is* something wrong," I said. "But I don't know what it is. Something's making me restless, discontent. I can't eat, I can't concentrate. My mind wanders, even on stage. And it's hard for me to sleep. I was up until five last night, staring at the shadows on the ceiling."

"Till five," you murmured sympathetically.

"Yes," I said. "But I suppose insomnia's an occupational disease among The Glorious Ones. Haven't you heard them, Pietro? Pantalone cries in his sleep, Armanda sings hymns, Brighella blathers about God and His holy angels. And Andreini thrashes and shouts as if he were fighting off demons. Haven't you heard them?"

Yet the moment I asked, I realized you hadn't. You weren't like the others; you slept soundly, every night. That was why I liked you.

"Yes," I repeated, "till five."

"Sounds like pregnancy to me," you laughed. (But was there a strange look in your eye, as if you knew the truth? Was I, the woman famous for her imagination, just imagining it? It seemed important to me, to know.)

"Can't you see it in me, Pietro?" I asked you. "The others notice it, I can tell. It's making them wary of me, they're standing back and watching. Columbina keeps asking me what's wrong. And it's scary, because it reminds me of my first days in the troupe, when they all thought I was crazy."

"Why did they think you were crazy?" you asked. "Because you were so beautiful?"

So you thought I was beautiful, Pietro. You probably thought it meant nothing to me, hearing you say it. After all, you'd heard kings call me beautiful. You'd seen princes slobbering over me like children at a bakery. You'd listened to Andreini praise my beauty every time he introduced the troupe.

But I never heard it, Pietro. I never saw it, I never believed it. Listen:

The first time Francesco came to my home, he amused my family by drawing little caricatures of us all. The sketch he drew of me was not really unkind; after all, he was courting me. Yet still, I felt as poor Armanda must have felt, when Flaminio proclaimed her ugliness before the convent. And that night, when I looked into the mirror, I saw the face of a hideous brown toad, bug-eyed, covered with warts.

We never believe we're beautiful, no matter how many times we hear it. We never believe it until someone says it in the right way.

Yet I believed you when you said it, Pietro. My knees felt weak; I couldn't talk. Even here, in heaven, a spirit without a body, I can still feel the excitement.

"Why did they think you were crazy?" you repeated. "Because you were so beautiful?"

"No," was all I could reply. "Not because I was beautiful. Because I was crazy."

Then, I got up, and left the tent.

So that was what happened. Nothing. That was what I told you. Nothing. I wanted to say that I'd rather be there with you than anywhere else on earth. I wanted to spend time with you, to explain the truth about myself, from beginning to end.

And I didn't say it.

But perhaps I can now. Perhaps there's time. Sleep, try to sleep, and I will do my best.

I wasn't born in a convent, the way Andreini always claimed. He only said it to scare Flaminio, to weaken the old man's will by reminding him of some crazy witch's curse.

How could any of them have believed it? How could I ever have learned the things I knew in a convent? How could I have mastered those hard-learned tricks, those skills, that ability to please and charm, had I not had so much practice, pleasing my parents?

As a child, I learned to sing, to dance, to play the lute. When guests came to dinner, I recited stanzas of terrible doggerel I'd composed myself. I was precocious, horribly spoiled, but my parents encouraged me. They knew that I needed those talents, in order to protect myself.

For there was something else in me which disturbed them more.

Every evening, my parents took me for a walk through the city, to display their newest jewel. In honor of these occasions, they dressed me in a green velvet gown. My mother put on her Chinese brocade cape. My father picked up his ivory-headed cane, and his Spanish leather pouch, full of coins.

The coins were for the beggars, who surrounded us constantly, reaching out their filthy hands, pointing to their goiters, pinching their skinny babies to make them cry. At such times, my father would take a coin from his purse, and hand it to me. He wanted me to have the satisfaction of presenting it to the beggars, of watching them mumble politely and shuffle away.

But one night, as we entered the main plaza, a ragged boy came running towards us. He raced across the square, then threw himself down on the ground at our feet.

"Here," said my father, unaccustomed to such extreme displays. "Take this penny, and go away."

But the beggar wouldn't move. Crouched on the ground, he looked up at me, so that I could see the tears streaming down his face.

"No!" he cried. "I want more! I want it all!"

Grumbling with disgust, my father took my hand, and tried to steer us away. But suddenly, a strange feeling came over me. I began to scream, to flap my arms in the air. And then, for the first time, I began to squawk like a duck.

"Give it to him!" I shrieked. "Give him all the money!"

Hoping to avoid a scandalous scene, my father dumped the contents of his pouch on the ground, and dragged us off. All the way home, neither of my parents spoke. But later that night, my mother called me to her room.

"Isabella," she whispered, stroking my hair. "You are too

young to understand this now. Still, I must tell you: already, you are a little crazy, and your heart is a little too generous. You must be careful, for such things are not always wise in a woman. They can make you very unhappy."

So that was why they encouraged my talents—so that I could protect those other parts of me. And I learned my tricks well. By the time Francesco started coming to my home, I'd learned them perfectly. And, while he courted me with those wonderful stories, I used them, every one. I charmed him, pleased him, delighted him; I did my best to weave a spell.

It was an old trick, Pietro, a joke. You've seen the Inamorata do it on stage, a thousand times. I wanted Francesco to love me, to take me with him, to let me join the troupe. But I made him think it was his own idea.

That is a trick most women know, Pietro; already, at sixteen, our acting is that good.

Now, looking down from heaven, I suddenly see: in a way, Francesco was telling the truth. My home might just as well have been a convent.

For that's how I looked at it, when I lay awake in my bed, staring out the window at the moon, praying that Francesco would rescue me. And on that night when he finally rode up to my window, and I climbed out of my elegant bedroom onto the back of his stallion—no nun could have been happier to leave her cold stone cell.

That night was magical, Pietro. There was a full moon in the sky. And, as I rode along behind Francesco, I felt as if we were riding into the moon, the way I'd heard poets sing of it, in love ballads.

We were married by a local priest, who made some bad joke about Andreini's unruly hair. But I hardly heard him. I was asleep, in a dream, riding the moon above the earth.

That night, I slept with Francesco for the first time. It wasn't like I thought it would be. "Is that it?" I wondered, lying beside him afterwards. "Surely, there's more to it than that." I was sure there was more to it, so I told myself it would probably change with time. And I fell asleep.

But the next morning, when I awoke, I knew that my dream was over. When Francesco gave that preposterous speech about me, and drew off my cloak, I found myself staring into the faces of The Glorious Ones, the faces of strangers. And suddenly, I was staring at them, and at myself, as if I'd risen a million miles into the air, and was looking down from heaven.

I saw it clearly, face to face. I saw it all. I was married to Francesco Andreini until the day of my death. I was an actress, touring with The Glorious Ones. And these complete strangers were my new family—these freaks, these dwarfs, these maniacs were my life.

I was no longer a young girl in my parents' house, dreaming about the adventurous life I would be leading with Francesco Andreini. I was actually leading that life, and it terrified me.

Suddenly, all my skills, all my tricks, all my talents deserted me. I couldn't help myself; I began to scream. I quacked and squawked like a duck.

Because that was my natural voice—the true voice of my craziness, and my generous heart.

Francesco never understood. At the time, he was confused, concerned, solicitous. But later, when I was better again, and I tried to explain, he refused to listen. He accused me of having faked the whole thing, just to throw him off balance.

"After all," he'd say. "You knew it beforehand. You had it all written out, in the play."

"Yes, I wrote it," I agreed. "But I *didn't* know. Hasn't that ever happened to you, Francesco? You write something which you think has nothing to do with you, and yet it comes true? Don't you know what I mean?"

"No," he replied. "I always see ahead. I always know how things will turn out. And you do too, Isabella, though you're too clever to admit it."

But he was wrong. I didn't know it would happen to me; and, once it did, I didn't know what to do. All I could do was shout and squawk. My spirit had left my body, and I couldn't get it back. I couldn't come close to anything, I couldn't touch anyone, I couldn't talk.

Finally, the Doctor began to give me opium, and it helped. At least, the fear was gone, and I could dream in peace.

Yet over and over, I had the same vision. I took to staring at the moon, for that was where I saw it.

I saw the dream of my childhood, the dream of that convent girl who lay awake and gazed at the moon. I saw the dream of that night Francesco Andreini rescued me from my parents' house.

And that was the reason I stared at the moon so longingly—I was trying to get back into my dream. But the moon had its eyes closed; it wouldn't look at me.

Then slowly, very slowly, I began to stop caring. Gradually, I began to notice the signs: I was feeling better, I could recognize the traces of my old self.

How strange, that it should have taken the Doctor's hot breath on my neck to finally awaken me. He was like that god, bringing his chick-pea child to life. But that was the way it happened.

One night, while the Doctor was assaulting me with some absurd sexual proposition, I turned my eyes from the moon, and saw the plain truth—despite myself, I still remembered all those little skills, those talents, that ability to please. And they still worked. They'd worked on the Doctor, on Pantalone, Columbina, Armanda, Francesco. They'd worked on titled aristocracy, on people with money, on the King of France! How blind of me, not to have noticed!

Soon, I felt whole again. I became confident. I began to take pleasure in my writing, my acting, my singing, in all the things I'd learned to do. I began to look around me, to enjoy the fame, the wealth, the success. The Doctor became my admirer, Colum-

FRANCINE PROSE

bina my friend; I made Pantalone and even Brighella come to like me. And I began to love The Glorious Ones.

Francesco and I became lovers; gradually, our love changed to that of husband and wife. And it was comfortable, it was good. We were kind to each other, we helped each other with the work. We fought and argued, like all married people, yet there seemed to be love in it. I had no reason to complain.

Sometimes, as I played opposite Francesco, I'd stop for a moment, and stand back. "These are the hours I'll look back on when I'm old," I thought to myself. "I'll remember them as my happiest times, the times when my life shone with light."

But now, looking back, I see I was mistaken: there's no light shining from those hours. All I can see is that something was wrong, right from the start. And it was this.

I worshiped Francesco too much. Though I'd tricked him into marrying me, I still believed he was infallible. Though I wrote the plays, starred in the dramas, won the audiences' hearts, I still looked up to him, as if he were my superior. I worshiped him, as if he were divine.

And indeed, with his strange monologues, his two sides, his half-wild feline nature, he seemed as mysterious and unknowable as a god.

I had complete faith in him, in his vision, his ability to predict the future. I was under his direction, I did as he said, I even tortured poor old Flaminio, for his sake.

Francesco was a hero to me. I was so pleased, so flattered, every time the hero wanted to sleep in my bed. And, just as I'd thought, it got better. I began to like it more, to let myself feel the pleasure. But still, there was something wrong: you can't make love to a god, it's not right. It's not like making love, it's like going to church. There's no room in the bed, for a mortal woman, and a god.

So I knew that there was something wrong. Yet I would never have known what it was if Flaminio Scala hadn't shown me the way.

126

One night, as I sat in Columbina's tent, she told me the story of her love affair with the Captain, twenty years before. She tried to pretend that it was all in the past, that she didn't care about him any more, that she pitied him. But I knew the truth.

I began to feel a certain uneasiness, a physical longing, like shivers. "That's what I want," I thought. "Plain human love. I'm tired of worshiping a god. I want something different, better. I want an ordinary man, with a mortal body, and a loving heart."

That night, when I returned to my tent, I couldn't sleep.

Now, looking down from this place where the angels are so clear-sighted that I long for the smoke of hell, I begin to understand.

I see what a clever trickster Flaminio was; though we never suspected, he was much better than Francesco. And I see that Columbina's story was but the first of his many tricks, of those tricks he continued to play on us from beyond the grave.

For, in giving Columbina that taste of human love, that story she remembered all her life, Flaminio had unsettled me. He was telling me about a kind of love I'd never dreamed of, on those nights I lay awake in my parents' house. It was something I wanted, even more than I wanted the moon.

And that was the beginning of my discontent.

But, at the time, I said nothing. How could I have explained myself? Francesco was the last one I could talk to. Even Columbina would never have understood.

So I tried to ignore it. I concentrated on my acting, my writing. I told myself that I should be grateful for my marriage. I had a good life, better than most people had. It was, as Francesco said in that funeral oration, a blessing from God.

Yet God has a way of revoking His blessings, as soon as we begin to see them as our rightful due. And that is just what happened.

For, on the night of Flaminio Scala's death, all my contentment suddenly disappeared. And all my love for Francesco Andreini turned to anger, and fear.

It's hard, Pietro, talking to you about Flaminio. He was dead before you joined the troupe, you never knew him. And God knows what you've heard about him from the others.

I myself never knew him well. I didn't even meet him until late in his life, when he was already weakened, damaged by Francesco. I never saw him at his best, at the height of his career—when, according to Columbina, his gaze could jolt the audience like a thunderbolt. In those last few weeks before his death, I got a hint of what he must have been like, and it was awesome. But I never really knew.

Still, I liked the Captain. As soon as I was well enough to tell one actor from another, I began to feel an odd affection for him. There seemed to be certain likenesses between us, though I didn't really know what they were. Only now do I see.

Neither of us were practical people, like Andreini. We were both hopeless dreamers, and his case was just as serious as mine: he had immortality on his mind; I wanted the moon. And we were similar in another way, which I couldn't identify until I saw it in you, Pietro; you share the same magic.

Yet my affection for the Captain was always mixed with pity; I felt sorry for him, even before he'd lost all his power. For the cards were stacked against him from the start. He was doomed to be alone. The others could never really have loved him, he didn't have a chance.

They were furious at him—furious at those horrible parts he'd cast them in. They hated him for those rules, those caricatures of themselves. They wanted *him* to die, too.

I remember how strangely they behaved at the Captain's funeral. They seemed completely out of character, the very opposite of their normal selves. Brighella was kind and solicitous; he held our hands to comfort us, and spoke of eternal life. Pantalone doled out fistfuls of gold, to finance the Captain's wake. The Doctor seemed meek and humble. And Armanda, who insisted on delivering Flaminio's eulogy, revealed a woman of passion and deep intelligence beneath that clownish mask.

I'd have thought they'd gone crazy, if I hadn't understood. They were flaunting it in the Captain's face, forcing his spirit to witness. "Look!" they were saying. "We're not those people we play on stage. You were wrong about us, Captain. You didn't know us."

Yet the very next day, they were their old familiar selves again. And they blamed the Captain for it, just as most men blame God. That was why I pitied Flaminio.

But at the time, I couldn't let that pity stop me. For the part I was to play opposite Flaminio Scala had already been written out. I was to help Francesco subvert him, weaken him, destroy his will. I was to help my husband bring about his downfall.

I played my part well, Pietro. I never faltered. Even at the moment of Flaminio's death, I never allowed a sign of sympathy or regret to cross my face. As I quenched Flaminio's last hope, as I raised the axe to finish off that dying bull, I was absolutely unrepentant, calm, controlled.

But, later that night, Flaminio Scala began to play another of his nasty tricks. Before his corpse had grown cold, the Captain's ghost began its vengeance.

Flaminio's body had just been taken from the stage. Francesco went off to make the funeral arrangements. And I returned to my tent, hoping to get some rest, to erase that frightful spectacle from my mind.

But I couldn't rest. There was something bothering me, something besides the shock of the Captain's death. There was something important which I couldn't remember, which I needed to know.

I thought for a long time, trying to figure out what it was. And then, suddenly, I felt Flaminio's spirit possess me. I felt him take hold of my mind, and lead it through the corridors of my memory. At last, his spirit paused, and opened the door of a dark chamber. And at that moment, I knew.

Long ago, when Francesco was courting me with his stories, he told me a peculiar anecdote. It concerned an unsuccessful actor—poor, unrecognized, down on his luck. One day, the actor accepted the sad fact that he would never find immortality through his art. So he decided to kill himself, in the middle of a performance, in a last heroic grasp at eternal fame.

"Francesco!" I thought to myself, the moment I remembered. "You knew it! You knew it in advance! Is that what you meant by foresight, by knowing the ends of things? If you knew it, why didn't you try to stop it? Or did you plan it that way, did you plan the Captain's death? If these are the sort of plans you make, Francesco, then what are your plans for me?!"

Now, it seems so foolish: I was like one of those crazy monks, driven to despair by the sudden realization that God has allowed evil to enter the world. But that night no one could have told me it was foolish.

I left the tent, and walked out into the night. For three hours, I paced through the camp, raging at Francesco in my mind. I felt betrayed, as if I'd married a villain, a monster, Satan himself. I despised him, and I was mortally afraid. I decided what I would say to him, I rehearsed it, word for word. I planned out my last scene, my accusation, my farewell.

"How clever of Flaminio," I thought, "to take his vengeance so soon, while his corpse is still warm."

But that night, when I returned to the tent and found Francesco already there, I began to see that the Captain's revenge wasn't yet over. And it was much, much crueller than I'd imagined.

As soon as I looked at Francesco, I became confused: was the Captain the one who'd died? Or was it my husband?

For there was no life left in Francesco's body. There was no light in his eyes. He seemed like a corpse, an empty hull, a dried-out kernel.

I began to accuse him. I tried to say the things I'd been rehearsing in my mind all night. But he didn't have the spirit to fight with me. He no longer loved me enough to make it worthwhile.

"How clever of Flaminio," I thought, "to have taken my husband's spirit with him to the other world."

And it was true. All at once, I realized: Francesco's whole life had been centered around that struggle with the Captain. Everything had come from it—his skill, his talent, his love for me. That love and hate for Flaminio were the only real feelings he'd ever had.

At the moment of Flaminio's death, Francesco's life had left him. I was married to a corpse.

My heart sank; my accusations crumbled. So what if Francesco had foretold the Captain's death? What good had it done him?

"Francesco," was all I could say, "is this how well you foresee the consequences of things?"

The death of love is terrible, Pietro; sometimes, I think it's worse than physical death. We were lucky that I died when I did. For, if you ever loved me, you can think of me now with the sweetest memories, the fondest regrets. But if I were still alive, and we stopped loving one another, it would be much, much sadder.

After the death of love, the corpse is always with you, filling the air with a rotten smell. You can't touch it, you can't talk to it. You can't kill it, and it won't go away.

That's how it was with Andreini and me. He was no longer a god to me, no longer a hero. Except when he was directing me on stage, we barely spoke. We never laughed together, we never discussed our work. And, though we shared the same bed, we rarely made love. Our hearts had dried up. Our bodies had turned to stone.

Perhaps you never saw him that way, Pietro. By the time you joined the troupe, he'd healed himself enough to project a show of competence. But I saw the difference. Brighella and Columbina spotted it right away. And by the end of that first year after the Captain's death even the audiences knew.

Every time Francesco and I played the Lovers together on stage, I heard impatient murmurs coming from the crowd. We had to shout out our lines, in order to be heard above the whispers, the coughs, the noise of crackling paper. The audiences couldn't accept us as the Lovers any more. The truth was too obvious. They couldn't be deceived.

So something had to change.

Francesco was beside himself. This was a consequence he'd never foreseen. He didn't know what to do. So he tried to pretend that nothing was happening.

But, one by one, all The Glorious Ones perceived the truth. And they were delighted to see Francesco caught unprepared.

At last, after a particularly unsuccessful performance, Armanda Ragusa spoke out. "Your role is wearing thin, Andreini," she said, tapping her finger against his chest. "What business did you have playing the Lover in the first place? You should have left the role to Flaminio, who was so good at it. What did you ever know about love?"

"Go to hell, Armanda," replied Francesco. "You were always on Flaminio's side. Your opinions on this subject are worthless."

But Francesco knew that Armanda was right: he and I could no longer play the Lovers together.

The next morning, Francesco announced his desire to assume the role of the Captain. Then, he went out in the street, to find a new actor to play the Lover's part.

You were the one he came back with, Pietro. Remember that afternoon? I emerged from my tent to find my husband standing with his arm around your shoulders, telling the others why he had chosen you.

"Ladies and gentlemen," he proclaimed, "may I introduce to you Pietro Visconti. He is a professional, this boy—not a rank amateur, like we were when we first joined The Glorious Ones. For twenty-seven years, he's been living by his wits, on the streets. He's recited verse, sung ballads, performed small skits for whatever he could get. He's rented his voice to merchants who wanted their products advertised in the alleyways. He's even dabbled in a bit of confidence trickery, this clever fellow. And whenever his luck ran out he disguised himself as a beggar, and played the part to perfection.

"He will make an ideal Lover, my friends. He is so handsome, he'll make the ladies break into cold sweats. He is so magnetic, he'll make them faint dead away. He has talent, experience— and, despite his age, he seems to know his way around."

That's what my husband said about you, Pietro. Remember?

He was lying. Flaminio would have cast the ideal lover to play the Lover's part; that was something the Captain would have done. But my husband's motives were exactly the opposite.

He didn't want you to be the ideal lover, Pietro. He didn't want you to be the kind of man I could ever love. He didn't want that to happen, he couldn't take that chance.

Of course, you never knew. Telling you seemed like an unnecessary cruelty. I suppose we could have laughed about it later, when I'd fallen in love with you, and proven Francesco wrong. But by then it was already too late. I came to your tent, and couldn't speak.

I saw Francesco's true motives, right away. How can I explain? There was something about your physical presence which he thought I'd consider beneath me. Your frame was broad; your body seemed solid, heavy. It wasn't that you looked like a peasant—how could a street actor have eaten well enough to resemble a peasant?

But there was a strange looseness in your arms and legs; your limbs weren't sinewy, like Francesco's. Your skin wasn't alive with raw nerve endings. And your eyes didn't burn like his once did. They were calm, clear blue, a little sleepy; there was no fire in them.

That was why Francesco thought I couldn't love you. Didn't he realize that I'd been burned in that fire long enough?

I looked at you for a long time, that first day. Idly, I wondered if you were the one who would give me human love. Then, suddenly, as I stared at you, the blood stopped running in my veins.

"Francesco!" I thought. "Not only can't you see the future—you also cannot see the past!"

For, at that moment, I saw that you were the beggar, Pietro, the same one who'd thrown himself at my parents' feet so long ago! I recognized your face; it was unmistakable. You were the one who'd demanded all the money in the pouch.

You had already claimed my generous heart.

Right then, I knew that we were witnessing the final act of Flaminio Scala's clever revenge. The Captain had trained my husband well. He'd taught him how to cast the roles. And, no matter what Francesco did, Flaminio's spirit was still in control.

Despite himself, Andreini had found the perfect Lover in you, Pietro. You played the part in life, just as you did on stage.

You had already stolen my father's ducats. Now you had come back for his daughter.

Now do you remember, Pietro? Do you remember that evening when you threw yourself on the ground? Probably not. What difference does it make?

And that's just what I told myself at the beginning, when I started to play opposite you. "What difference does it make?" I thought. "What does it matter that I met this man before, many years ago?"

When we rehearsed our scenes together, I concentrated on my acting. I tried to regard you as another actor, a talented newcomer, nothing more. I tried not to see you as a likely source of human love. My life would have made that love too complicated; it could never have been the simple thing I desired. And I wanted to keep my life simple. So I kept my distance.

But you know the old story. You've seen it, in every one of the plays.

I began to think about you constantly. I thought how much I liked you—you seemed so sensible, so funny, so kind. I began to laugh and joke with you; I began to wonder what it would be like to sleep with you. After awhile, you were always on my mind. When I praised you on stage, I meant every word.

At last, I realized that I'd fallen in love. You'd won my generous heart, you'd charmed my craziness. For the second time, you'd spoken to my natural voice—the voice that shouted and squawked.

A few days later, I discovered I was pregnant.

Wait, Pietro. I see you wincing in your sleep. I know what's running through your mind. You're afraid that I'll say something silly, that I'll claim the baby was fathered by the power of love. Rest easy. I'm not that kind of woman. I know the simple facts of nature. I couldn't believe such nonsense.

And yet, I've always wondered if perhaps the opposite was true. Was that why none of the The Glorious Ones had ever fathered or conceived a child? None of them had ever really loved, not even Armanda or Columbina; for there was always hate in it. Is that what made them sterile?

And why, after ten years of marriage, using no precautions, should I suddenly conceive Andreini's child? Why, when he and I had only slept together twice that spring? It was love which opened the doors of my womb, Pietro. What else could explain it?

I mean it metaphorically, of course. Because it couldn't have been your child. On that day I came to your tent to offer myself, I couldn't even speak. I was afraid that I'd disgrace myself; I'd ask you, and be rejected. I didn't believe you loved me, I thought I was imagining those long looks of yours.

Now, looking back, it seems so strange. I was Isabella

Andreini, the greatest actress and playwright in all Europe. And you turned me back into a sixteen-year-old girl, with much less nerve than I'd had at sixteen. It was that odd sensation of becoming a virgin again. You know, Pietro: the poets speak of it.

And I know how you did it.

That was the likeness I spoke of before, the tie that bound you, me, and Flaminio. There was something we shared in common: we were the ones with whom everyone fell in love.

And it was all because we were such dreamers. We lived so close to our own imaginations, we'd learned how to reach in and play with other people's dreams. We made them believe that we loved them; at the very same time, we made them think our love was all in their minds, a fantasy of their own creation. It confused them, made them unsteady, afraid. In that way, we bewitched them, and pulled them into our web. It was the source of much of our power.

Flaminio knew those tricks. He played them on Armanda, on Columbina. No wonder those women loved him so much. I'd learned them long ago, so that I could work my magic on Francesco, on The Glorious Ones, on the King of France himself. And you, Pietro? You did it to me.

Yet we never meant to harm anyone. It wasn't our fault. For the truth of the matter was that we never knew what we really felt, and what was just in our imaginations.

But on that afternoon I visited you in your tent, I knew exactly what I felt. That was why I was so frightened.

That was why I couldn't speak.

Two days after we reached Lyons, the pains began. Early in the morning I opened my eyes to see the velvet canopy in my bedroom at the king's palace. Then, I looked down, and saw the bloodstains on the white satin sheets.

"Columbina!" I cried. "Quick! Get help!"

And that was when I knew The Glorious Ones were going to kill me. Columbina moved sluggishly, like an old woman. It took her almost an hour to fetch Francesco from the dining room, where he was breakfasting with the nobles. They entrusted me to the Doctor's care—Graziano, who knew nothing about medicine! Pantalone quibbled about the pennies needed to buy me infusions, herbs, and leeches. Brighella and Armanda stood outside my room, fighting constantly, sapping my strength with their racket.

And Francesco? Francesco refused to let me see you. So he must have known, he must have noticed how I'd watched you, during those last months.

"No," he insisted, ignoring all my pleas. "That one will make you worse. He's as unruly as a child, as clumsy as a bull. He won't know how to behave at an invalid's bedside."

So I lay there, praying to Mary. I thought that, as a woman, she would understand. "Please," I begged her. "Let me get well. Let me get well so that I can go to Pietro and tell him. Don't let me die, so he'll never know."

But I'd forgotten. The Blessed Mother was a virgin. She couldn't understand. She wouldn't grant my prayer.

So that is why I'm coming to you in this dream. That is why I'm returning, from beyond death, from beyond the gates of heaven, from beyond that state funeral, financed by the King of France. I want to tell you what was in my heart, I want you to know. If necessary, I'll shout at you. I'll scream and squawk, in the true voice of my spirit. But I want you to understand.

Wait. The blankets have slipped down to your waist, and I'm afraid you'll be awakened by the chill. Lie still, sleep, for now it's time to tell you about heaven.

There is a window in the sky, Pietro, through which the angels can look down and see the future of the world. That was where I met Flaminio Scala again, after so many years. He was standing at the window, with his nose pressed against the pane.

But he couldn't see. Poor Flaminio, even in heaven he couldn't see the ends of things. He saw vague outlines, blurred shapes; but he couldn't see the details.

"Isabella!" he cried, greeting me warmly. "All is forgiven! I, Flaminio Scala, the most humble and charitable angel in heaven, assure you that all is forgiven. Now please, quickly, do me a favor. Look through this window, and tell me what you see!"

I look through the window. And I see. I see the end of The Glorious Ones. I see them dying, one by one. I see their deaths enacted, as if each one were a short scenario.

I see the Doctor growing older, more senile. At last, in the course of his demented research, he drinks a bottle of his own medicine, for experimental purposes. And the medicine is rat poison.

I see Brighella, slipping from a high scaffolding, landing on the stage. His neck is bent back, askew, like that of a broken doll. When he comes up to heaven to collect his final reward, Saint Peter is waiting for him at the gate.

"Brighella," says the saint, "fifty years ago, our Precious Lord resolved to break your neck on the gallows, to consign you to the pits of hell. There was, however, a mistake; such things happen, even in heaven. But now, He has decided to amend His oversight."

As the saint falls silent, Brighella begins to fly through the air like a maddened gadfly. He falls and tumbles, buzzes through the clouds. Then, he vanishes out of sight.

I see Pantalone growing sicker, more obsessed. I see him being buried in a plain wooden coffin, with a gigantic sack of gold beneath his head.

I see Columbina living to an old age, then dying from an unexpected recurrence of the French pox.

I see you too, Pietro. One night, a rich young widow comes out of the crowd. You sleep with her; she likes it, and proposes marriage. You become her husband, and no longer have to beg in the streets. You die of gout, a rich man's disease.

Don't pity me, Pietro, for having to watch you with another woman. It makes it easier to be here, away from you, in heaven.

I try and try to see Francesco's future, but I can't. I, too, have my blind spots. Though perhaps it's because Flaminio's already stolen my husband's spirit, and taken it with him to heaven; perhaps Francesco's soul is already here, and I just can't find it.

And, at the very end, I see something which makes me glad that Flaminio is so blind.

I see you writing down this dream, Pietro, and giving it to Armanda, who's begged you to do it. I see her putting it together with the broadsides, the posters, the copies of the plays, with all the histories the others have written. I see her assembling them, as a monument to Flaminio Scala, to insure the Captain's immortality.

She begins to carry this strange collection around with her, day after day, month after month, year after year. She carries the papers in a pouch on her back, like an artificial hump. They are never more than a few feet from her side.

But gradually, an odd thing starts to happen. As Armanda grows older, she feels the pouch growing heavier and heavier. It becomes so heavy that she can't move while she's wearing it. She can't lift it. It's crippling her, crushing her bones, ruining her life.

Yet she can't abandon it; she's promised Flaminio Scala.

One day, staggering beneath her impossible pouch, she stumbles towards the river. Still wearing that monument to Flaminio on her back, she walks into the water.

Armanda's body begins to float downstream. And the leaves of the manuscript float out around her, spinning on the surface of the water, like lily petals.

So it came true! That old witch, Flaminio Scala's mother, had told the truth! Flaminio *was* undone, condemned to obscurity, by a woman from the convent, the one he'd adopted himself. His name was obliterated by that harmless little dwarf, who loved him so much, and who was so undone by him.

When I turned my back on that scene, I couldn't look at Flaminio. There were tears in my eyes.

"What did you see?" he demanded. "Tell me: what did you see?"

"Captain," I replied. "I saw wonders. I saw the entire future of the theater. I saw millions of stages all over the world. I saw brilliant playwrights, great actors. I saw thousands of troupes—which would never have existed if not for you and your Glorious Ones."

"But what about me?" he asked. "Did you see my name, enthroned in glory for eternity?"

"I couldn't see the details," I said, very softly. "All I could see were the vague, blurred shapes."

Muttering to himself, Flaminio walked away. And, as I stood there, gazing after him, I suddenly remembered an interlude we played, in that first drama, so long ago, the one about the Moon Woman.

In the interlude, I played Pantalone's melancholy daughter, out walking in my father's garden. There was a bright moon in the sky, and I was gazing at my lover, the full moon.

Pantalone had filled his garden with marble statues, which gleamed eerily in the dim light. Dusted with white powder, standing perfectly still, every one of the Glorious Ones pretended to be a statue.

I looked at them all, one by one, frozen in that gleaming light. And, one night, I saw:

I saw them all—Flaminio, Armanda, Brighella, Pantalone, Francesco, Columbina, the Doctor. I saw their whole lives, their pasts, their souls, their dreams about themselves. It was as if I'd invented them, like characters in a play.

I saw them gleaming, petrified in marble. And I began to wonder: what sort of play is this which I have written? Is it really a comedy, as we'd always said? Or is it actually a tragedy?

At that moment, the statues came to life. The Glorious

Ones jumped down from their pedestals and surrounded me. Armanda and Brighella leapt into the air. Francesco turned amazing cartwheels, the Doctor puffed out his chest, Flaminio flourished his sword. All of them danced around me, in a circle, as I stared up at the moon.

Then, suddenly, I knew beyond a doubt: it was indeed a comedy.

Here in heaven, they have their own answer to that question.

Perhaps this will surprise you, Pietro, but many of the angels are actors. That is what they do with their spare time. Every day, all over heaven, thousands of short skits are performed, each one based on a true incident which took place on earth. All the great stories are played out—legends from the Greeks, from the Bible, the masterpieces of the Orient, and an astonishing number of wonderful stories which have never been written down.

Eventually, all the newcomers to heaven begin to notice a surprising thing: many of the stories are the same, most of the dramas seem interchangeable. There are vast millions of Isabellas, Brighellas, Flaminios—all wearing different costumes, all living in different times.

As soon as the new angels realize this, their wings begin to shimmer with joy. "That's all human life is about," they tell each other happily. "It's just a series of stories and plays, most of which are exactly the same!"

Immediately, they forget the sorrow of their own stories, the ones they've lived out on earth. "That is the meaning of heaven," they say. "The knowledge that it is all just a story. Surely, *this* is what Jesus meant, when He promised that we would be cleansed of the memory of mortal pain!"

Sometimes, I agree with them, and it comforts me; the thought of The Glorious Ones no longer causes me such suffering.

But sometimes, I'm not so sure; I wonder. Because if they are right, Pietro, if everything that befell The Glorious Ones is all just another story, then tell me, tell me this:

Why does Flaminio still long for worldly immortality? And why am I bothering to come to you, in this dream?

ABOUT THE AUTHOR

Francine Prose is the author of sixteen novels, including *A Changed Man*, winner of the Dayton Literary Peace Prize, and *Blue Angel*, a finalist for the National Book Award. Her most recent works of nonfiction include the highly acclaimed *Anne Frank: The Book, the Life, the Afterlife*, and the *New York Times* bestseller *Reading Like a Writer*. A former president of PEN American Center and a member of the American Academy of Arts and Letters, as well as the American Academy of Arts and Sciences, Prose is a highly regarded critic and essayist, and has taught literature and writing for more than twenty years at major universities. She is a distinguished writer in residence at Bard College, and she lives in New York City.

Open Road Integrated Media is a digital publisher and multimedia content company. Open Road creates connections between authors and their audiences by marketing its ebooks through a new proprietary online platform, which uses premium video content and social media.

CPSIA information can be obtained at www.ICGtesting.com
Printed in the USA
BVOW01s0721261213

340165BV00002B/27/P

9 781480 445420